KIM

KIM

ROBERT COLBY

WILDSIDE PRESS

CHAPTER ONE

It was a Monday afternoon in February. The tourist season was in full swing along the streets and boulevards of Miami. There were so many out-of-state Cadillacs that you could hardly find a Florida jalopy among them. Brooklyn was asking directions from Birmingham and by the time they understood each other, a Times Square cop couldn't have straightened out the jam behind them.

I was down in the lobby of the Dupont Plaza at the foot of Biscayne Boulevard. The Dupont is a combination hotel and office building, another of those modern jewels of architecture which finger the skyline with winking glass and shining stone, monuments to play in the Mecca of sun and fun.

It was a little after four and I had just come from my bimonthly clipping in the lobby barber shop. I had bought a paper at the newsstand and was striding towards the elevator bank with my eyes on the print, when a hand clutched my arm and I swung about.

She was a small woman and thin. She had shrewd dark eyes set deep in a narrow-pinched face. She had a wart on the right side of her chin and her face was pushed so close to mine I could see the single gray hair which appeared to sprout from the exact center of this wart. The hair on her head was also gray and pulled back sharply into a tight bun. And with her pointed nose and chin, she was a kind of weapon on a stick, poised to strike.

She looked to be late fiftyish and was of a type who had long ago lost all interest in concealing either age or ugliness. She wore what must have been an expensive blue silk with white polka dots, though it hung loosely on her scrawny figure. The one thing about her which fascinated me was the hand which still clutched my arm. Because one of its grasping talons was encircled by a ring which contained a diamond the size of a marble, this diamond emitting a luster of some fifty thousand candle power—at a dollar a candle.

"Are you Mr. Striker?" she said. "Mr. Rod Striker?"

"I'11 admit that much."

"Oh. Well, I was just on my way up to your office and asking directions when that man at the magazine stand pointed you out."

"I'll see that he's rewarded," I said. "One way or another."

"Yes. Well, I'm Mrs. Martha Rumshaw," she said challengingly.

"I'm sorry," I answered.

"Sorry! What on earth are you sorry about?"

"I mean, I'm sorry, but the name is not familiar."

She cocked her head and the fifty-thousand-dollar hand dropped from my arm. "I came to see you on a matter I would like to have investigated," she hurried on. "It's most urgent."

"Almost all the matters which come to us are urgent, Mrs. Rumshaw. Why don't you run up to the office with me and we'll discuss it."

"I don't like stuffy offices with that grim steel furniture," she said.

"Our offices are not stuffy, Mrs. Rumshaw. And we have no steel furniture. It's limed oak. And our carpets are so thick that once a woman took off her shoe in my office and it's never been found."

It was almost true. We catered to the well-heeled customers, often the ones who came down for the winter on their own yachts. We had a corner suite on the twelfth floor, overlooking the bay. It was last-word plush.

"Still," she said, "I'd prefer to talk to you over a drink.

I would have asked you to come out to the house but I couldn't reach you by phone and I was in a hurry. Isn't there a lounge?"

"A bar? Sure. Right in the building."

"Please take me there," she said. "I could use a drink."

We found a table at the back of the room where, with just a turn of the head, you could look out upon a blue green slice of the bay. Mrs. Rumshaw ordered a whiskey sour and I settled for a very dry martini.

She sat looking morosely out the window until she had taken the first long swallow of her drink. Then she leaned forward and said, "I have a niece. She's very pretty. She's beautiful. But she's only twenty-two. And reckless. Her mother and father were killed in a hotel fire years ago. Kim, that's her name, was visiting me at the time of the fire and I just took charge of her from then on. I was appointed her legal guardian. Her mother, my sister, was poor and I had a large fortune left me by my husband. So I gave Kim all the advantages which her own parents could never afford. We became very close and she even took my name. I sent her to the best schools, gave her a car, spending money. In fact, Mr. Striker, I've left her my entire estate—which amounts to over two million dollars. And now—"

"And now," I finished, "she's turned on you. She's running around with a man you don't approve of, some low money-grabbing character unworthy of her, a guy whose guts you hate."

"Oh, you're smart, Mr. Striker," she said. "You put things rather crudely, but you're smart. How did you guess?"

"I saw it coming. We have two or three cases like this a year." And looking at Mrs. Rumshaw, my sympathies were already leaning towards the girl, Kim.

"Well," she said, "you probably never had a case quite like this and you guessed wrong from the beginning. My niece is devoted to me," she said smugly. "And we see eye-to-eye on everything—including men!"

"But you just said—"

"I was baiting you, Mr. Striker. I adore tripping people who have the silly notion, after five minutes in my presence, that I'm the typical old-maid-aunt guardian who rules with a heavy hand, using great filthy wads of money as my whip."

I smiled, liking the woman a little better. "Okay," I said. "So I jumped to a conclusion. And you had your fun. But at your own expense. Because, as you'll find out, Mrs. Rumshaw, my time is valuable."

"I've heard you come high," said Mrs. Rumshaw. "But in this case, money is no object."

"That's good, very good. My favorite phrase. Money is no object. We'll get along fine. Now what's the real problem here?"

She had a cigarette stuck in the corner of her mouth and when I tried to light it, she brushed my hand away and flared an ordinary kitchen match on the bottom of the table. She inhaled and sent a giant cloud of smoke over my head.

"Actually," she said, "Kim is in love with a very fine young man by the name of Howard Massey. Howie is twenty-six, has an automobile dealership here in town and is a *real* man. I like him and even if I didn't, he's Kim's choice and that's enough for me. He's no blueblood, whatever that is, and I don't give a particular damn if a man's father was a garbage collector and his mother a scrub woman, as long as he came out of it with some mettle of his own."

"I'm beginning to like you, Mrs. Rumshaw."

She chuckled, dribbling smoke. "You didn't at first?"

"No."

"Why?"

"I don't like old biddies who go around lousing up little girls' lives like female Hitlers compensating for their own frustrations. I think little girls over eighteen should be allowed to louse up their own lives—within reason. In the beginning you impressed me as the type. I'm sorry."

"I can't help the way I look," she said. "When the good Lord passed out beauty, I was so far back in line there was nothing left but a few odd features nobody wanted. But when the window opened for spirit and determination, I was right up front!" She laughed, a sad little sound. "Say, you're a pretty outspoken sort, even for a private detective. Of course, I personally like a man who is frank. But don't you lose a lot of clients with that sharp tongue?"

"Mrs. Rumshaw," I said, "I run my own show because I never could eat the kind of exhaust piped out from the arrogant phonies you usually find in charge of simpering yes-men and fanny osculators. Sure, I lose a few clients now and then. The ones who would have been colossal pains anyway. But let's get back to your niece. She must be in trouble or you wouldn't be here."

"That's right," she said. "Now, I told you that Kim is reckless but I didn't mean it in the literal sense. She's fun-crazy and still a bit immature at times. Even though she loves Howard Massey and they're engaged and are to be married in April, she still refuses to conform to the extent of walling herself away from every other male in the universe until she actually is married. Occasionally, not very often, I'll admit, she does have a date or two. Howie is smart enough to be tolerant, even to pretend indifference, which makes him all the more intriguing.

"But a few weeks ago he had to fly to Detroit for a dealers' convention and he was gone several days. While he was away, Kim went to a party given by some people who live next door. And there she met a man by the name of Tarino, Eddie Tarino." She paused and looked at me expectantly.

I nodded. "Sure, I know Tarino. Not well, of course. We used to insult each other now and then when I was on the force. He owns a couple of clip joints, one on Biscayne and the other out west on Flagler. B-girl operation. The usual strip acts with the girls playing patsy with the johns between grinds. Tarino is a sharpie, an operator. But not a very bad boy—on the books."

"He also owns a yacht," she said. "A big yacht that he charters for cruises to the Bahamas." She said this with a raised eyebrow.

"All right, and what's wrong with that?"

"He supplies some of his party-girls for those cruises."

"Probably."

"And even I can guess what goes on a few miles out to sea."

"Checkers?"

"Hardly."

"We call it stateroom checkers. Mrs. Rumshaw, the world is a great big whirling den of sin and there are certain kinds that get more attention from the police than others. It's a public attitude. The public eye is inclined to wink at what it laughingly calls necessary evil."

"I also hear," said Mrs. Rumshaw behind another giant puff of smoke, "that they do a lot of gambling on those cruises. And God knows what else."

"Almost anything else, because who watches portholes in the middle of the Atlantic on dark nights? So how does this concern you and your niece, aside from the fact that she met Tarino at a party?"

"That's what I'm trying to tell you. While Howie was out of town, Kim went along on one of those week-end cruises. As Mr. Tarino's guest. She thought it would be exciting. And at the time I believed it was an entirely different kind of thing—I didn't know anything about Mr. Tarino. But now I suspect that Kim had an affair with the man."

"Well, that's too bad, if it's true. Maybe it taught her something. So now why don't you let her forget it?"

"I would. Oh, I'd be glad to. But this Tarino won't let her forget it."

"Blackmail?"

"No. Not at all. He simply fell in love with her—or whatever passes for love with his type. And now, although Kim simply loathes him, he won't let her alone. He forces her to go with him."

"Aw, c'mon now, Mrs. Rumshaw. Forces?"

"Yes. Forces."

"How?"

"Well, it's terribly insidious and subtle. He doesn't lay a hand on her or anything like that. He simply makes threats."

"He threatens her with harm?"

"No. He threatens to harm *me*. And especially Howard Massey. One night two strange men caught Howie in the parking lot behind his apartment house, just as he was getting out of his car in the pitch dark. And they beat him brutally without really leaving a mark. You know, body punches. And they warned him to stay away from Kim or next time they'd kill him."

I nodded, seeing the pattern of a sly form of terror, mostly by implication. "Did anyone ever threaten you personally, Mrs. Rumshaw?"

Her face darkened, her eyes flashed. "Yes! I got a phone call one night. A tough-sounding man said I would be beaten to a pulp if Kim stopped going with Eddie Tarino and that I would be found floating in the bay if she married Howard Massey."

"You didn't recognize the voice?"

"No, I didn't. It wasn't Tarino, though. I know what he sounds like."

"Probably one of his boys. Now—did you take this to the police?"

"Oh yes, of course."

"And what did they say?"

"They wanted evidence. Something in writing or a witness to these threats. Since we never got anything in the mail and since no one ever heard one of those threats but myself and Howie, and since we couldn't identify the persons making the threats, the police said that by law they were helpless to do anything."

"That's true. There must be evidence of some kind for them to act."

"I know, Mr. Striker, and that's why I came to you."

"Has Tarino ever passed any of these threats to your niece, Kim?"

"No. On the contrary. To her he denies them. He just keeps calling and she goes out with him because she's afraid for me and for Howard."

"Okay, I have the picture. Now what is it you want me to do that the police can't do?"

Her eyes walked over me, studying all that was visible of me above the table.

"You're a big man," she said. "Are you over six feet?"

"Six three."

"You look muscular," she said. "And hard. I mean your eyes. Sometimes your eyes are friendly, even warm. But they're hard, too. Know what I mean?"

"What are you trying to say, Mrs. Rumshaw?"

She turned for a moment to gaze out the window, her hand twirling the glass on the table so that in certain positions the sun caught that big diamond and made it do a little fire dance that set me to thinking of hard money and easy living. And vice versa. Then she turned back and her jaw was thrust out half a foot from the rest of her face.

"I'll give you five thousand dollars," she said. "And I'll hire the best lawyer money can buy if there's any trouble." Her lips, bleached of color, pressed in flat against her teeth. "But I want you to grab that man Tarino in some dark alley tonight and beat him until he begs for mercy and promises on his knees that he'll stop his threats and leave my niece alone!"

Even the wart on her chin was flushed, a tiny red beacon of anger. She poked a bony finger at my chest.

"That's what I want you to do, Mr. Striker. That's exactly what I want you to do."

CHAPTER TWO

Forty-five minutes later I was gazing out over the bay from Myra Bailey's third floor apartment on 23rd off Biscayne. Myra was clutching a drink, looking bemused and slowly stirring the air with one long pendulous leg as I told her of the woes of Mrs. Martha Rumshaw.

Myra is a partner in the agency. At least she has a one-third interest. She contributed a little money and a lot of special talent. She's twenty-nine and used to be a policewoman out in L.A. where she worked with Juvenile, Bunko and Vice at one time or another. This was before she decided, like me, that the royal road to a five-figure bank account led directly away from all city payrolls. We are both very practical types, having no stars in our eyes, worshiping no heroes and collecting no autographs except those of the Secretary of the Treasury on currency of the realm, large denominations preferred. We were in the P. I. racket not because we loved the work and wanted to use our knowledge to relieve suffering humanity of its burden of evil, but because we wanted to relieve the customers of as much goddamn money as the traffic would bear. If we gave one hell of a lot of dedication to the job and drew certain ethical lines which we never crossed, it was because we wanted to build a sweet reputation, hold our license and make still more of that same goddamn money than anyone else in the game. If that sounds just a little mercenary, don't blame me, it's that kind of a world, buddy. And I didn't create the system—I only want to beat it!

I'm thirty-four and while that's not very old, I've seen a lot of policewomen in my time. Some of them looked like lady wrestlers, some of them were chubby and some of them were walking bone assemblies. A few were fairly cute tricks and would cause you to look back casually over your shoulder for a second helping. But I never saw any knock-you-down, pop-your-eyes-out beauties in my corner of the world. Because it simply is not the sort of rat-race to attract beauty queens and other dames of similar construction.

But Myra Bailey, if not the prototype of Miss America, or Miss Soapsuds, or Miss Cornpone, is an exception. She has blonde hair the color sand takes in the moonlight—not that phony bleached Brillo stuff. Her hair is cut medium short and brushed back from her face, though she has bangs in two simple strands which dangle at either side of her forehead like parentheses. Her eyes are large and azure, reflecting alertness and composure in equal parts. She has a straight nose with nostrils delicately flared, an abundant mouth and high cheekbones in a full oval face. She wears little make-up and nothing about her is designed to clobber you over the head with a jazzy neon sexiness.

If you like Katharine Hepburn and other such slender etchings in bone, forget her. She has a lot upstairs in the balcony and though her waist is narrow, her hips are artfully generous. She looks taller than she is because she stands proudly, not with one of those apologetic slumps. Perhaps it is an attitude, because she has plenty which compels, but the total effect of her is subdued. In a party room full of gushing butterflies, she would be noticed, not for her social acrobatics, but for her very stillness.

"So Mrs. Rumshaw wanted you to go over and club this Tarino character into bloody submission," said Myra now. "And what did you tell her, Rod?"

"I said she could find half a dozen pugs for the job in one of those swing-and-sweat gyms around town. At twenty bucks a copy. I told her I don't hire out by the punch, I sell what's in my head."

"And how did that digest with her?" Myra tapped a toothpick-impaled olive against the rim of her glass, caused the olive to disappear in a curl of pink tongue behind flashing teeth of an excellence despised by all dental plumbers.

"She was surprised," I answered. "She said she had heard I was tougher than boarding-house steak. All because I smashed a few heads in those shiv-and-broken-bottle massacres when I was with homicide. So I said, 'Look, Mrs. Rumshaw, that was all nice and legal and in the course of duty. Part of the job—and they can have it. Those days are gone. I can give protection. I can defend. If a guy tries to beat up, cut up or shoot up a client, I can chop him down and I can chop with the best of them. But that's it. I have about as much license to assault and batter some Joe who seems to be minding his own business as any other citizen. And that's no license at all.'

"My God, that woman is naïve in a lot of ways. But she finally agreed that I might be able to handle Tarino by out-thinking him just as well. She doesn't care how we pull him him off her niece's neck as long as we do it."

"We?" said Myra, arching a brow.

"Sure," I said, and I had to smile. "Mrs. Rumshaw had heard about your special talents. From Lieutenant Ulrich, bless his ever-lovin'. Because he goosed her gold-plated bottom in our direction. Anyway, she thought maybe you could sidle up to Tarino and mud-dle-sex him into such a trance that he would forget all about Kim and her comparatively amateur attractions."

"Bro—ther!" said Myra. "You're kidding."

"No," I said, "For five thousand bucks, who's kidding?" I watched the long bend of one stockinged leg as it fell sleekly from beneath her skirt. And I thought how it had been a long time now. Better than three months. Even though my apartment was only a couple of sto-ries straight up, thirty seconds removed. Myra would run from me and hide behind her strictly-business façade the minute something happened to her which she called "getting emotionally involved."

"Not even for five thousand," said Myra, "will I play call girl for Mrs. Rumshaw. She can go to—and she can muddle-sex Tarino herself."

"You just ain't seen Mrs. Rumshaw," I said. "Of course I clued her right away. But don't worry, you'll earn your share."

"How?"

"Well, you don't have to sleep with the guy to get some informa-tion out of him. Just hypnotize him a little."

"What kind of information?"

I hiked away from the window and sat down, dragging deeply on my cigarette and pretending to look thoughtful while I studied Myra, enjoying the little nudge of desire she gave me, a nudge that would become a giant slam if I didn't resist.

"Well, Rod," she said. "Are you still there? Or have we been cut off?"

"I'm thinking," I muttered.

Cool, I mused. That was the outward quality of her. Everywhere you looked she was cool on the surface. Cool after three sets of tennis. Cool in the furnace of midsummer when the only wind was like the breath from a blow torch. Cool running or sitting. Cool in the tight squeeze of a dangerous situation. And in that poised exterior, frosty as a highball glass new from the freezer, lay her value as a partner. And her magnetism as a female. Because on those rare occasions when the ice thawed, Jesus God, she was a dancing fire in bed. And in between, if you knew how to look for it, you could see the flame in her eyes.

But she was not one of those stone faces. Never. She had many sides and she played many parts. She was adaptable. She could be the lady with the soft face and smile, the genteel voice. Or tough and knowing with the hoods. She could play a raucous tramp in a gin mill. She had a face and a sound for any occasion, but even when she was angry she seemed always cool. That was Myra Bailey.

"I'll tell you," I said. "About this information we'll need. About turning you loose on Tarino. I think we'll let you sit out for the first round. Then we'll see. Because first, I'm going over and talk with our boy Tarino myself. I'd like to look the bastard in the eye and see what makes him creep. Then, if he won't scare, we'll try something more subtle. We'll sneak up on him. We'll come in the back door. Let's play it that way."

Myra drew deeply on her cigarette and for moments said nothing. She had a way of looking directly at you during some of her little silences, her eyes so wide and unblinking that they seemed magnified, growing towards you from across the room. I have known people who found that stare uncomfortable, even unnerving. As if she were taking you apart mentally, inspecting the hidden garbage of your character with disdain. But I understood that she was not really seeing me, she was probing for answers with the clever scalpel of her mind.

"What's this Tarino like?" she said.

"Well, he's rather small and he's—"

"I don't give a square tire about his figure. I want the shape of his mind."

"Angular. It's full of angles, crazy angles. He can look at a bowling ball and see an angle. But I can't draw you a blueprint. Nothing much shows on the surface. The guy is smooth, a clam about nothing that would give you much of a hint. Hell, I only talked to him a couple of times. I got the impression he was a sneaky son-of-a-bitch."

Myra nodded. "Sneaky and imaginative," she said. "He's got a thing for this Kim. She can't be bought. He can't hold a gun on her, or twist her arm, or carry her off to his jungle and stay out of jail. So what does he do? Nothing—in person. But he has his goons threaten the boy friend—and Mrs. R. Then he puts on his poker face and with clubs up his sleeve he calls Kim and says, 'I'll be over at seven, baby.' And by God, she's ready and waiting at five minutes to. He doesn't even threaten her, personally. He's too smart for that. So what's the answer?"

"Ulrich has a recording on the phones," I said. "But that's as far as he can go for the time being."

"Whose phones?"

"The boy friend's, Howard Massey. And Mrs. Rumshaw's. Kim has her own nest. She insisted on being unchained from the old gal, to that extent."

"Ahhh, sweet liberty," said Myra. "At last I've found thee. No tape recorder on the girl's phone?"

"No need. No threats."

"Any strange voices recorded so far on the others?"

"Not word one," I answered. "The big silence set in right after the gimmicks were fixed to the phones."

Myra made a face of disgust, sighed. "What did Mr. Rumshaw do to pile up all that gold?"

"He was big in rum," I said.

"That's where he got his name?"

"You never heard of Shaw's rum?"

"Idiot! No, really?"

"Well, I was only half kidding. He had a giant slice of a distillery. He hailed from old Kain-tuck and his daddy, no, his grand-daddy, was a moonshiner. Honest Indian, he was. That's what aunty told me."

"Well, I don't care how he made it as long as we get a share," said Myra. "I'll give some thought to Tarino and company." She held up the cocktail shaker. "One for the road?"

I brought my empty glass to where she sat on the couch and plopped down beside her. "What road?" I said.

"That crazy road to Tarino's snake pit. I thought you were going over to see him." She took my glass and poured.

"Oh hell, it's early yet. He hangs upside down until dark and he's just now getting ready to fly out of his cave." I sneaked my arm around her and sipped my drink. "This stuff is almost warm," I said.

"And I suppose you're not."

"Not what?"

"Warm." She smiled her way-ahead-of-you smile. I put the glass on the table. My fingers walked down her shoulder and over the long hill of her breast. She pretended not to notice. She uncrossed her legs and silk stockings whispered of intimate secrets.

"It's been a long time, Myra," I said. And then I kissed her.

Her mouth opened and for one molten quarter of a minute there was the searching demand of her tongue, the taut cone of her breast thrust against my palm. And then she broke away and gave me a little-boy pat on the cheek before she stood, smoothing her skirt.

"I'm hungry," she announced.

"Aw, now listen, I'm hungry too!"

"I know," she said. "And it's been a long time. And that's good for you. Works up an appetite."

"Oh yeah? You think I'll go hungry? You think you set the only table in town?"

"Oh Rod," she sighed, and seemed to sag a little. I knew she was jealous, though usually she concealed it with a bland face or smart crack. But now she wore a slightly pained expression, for once her eyes were indecisive. So I thrust an arm about her and pulled her gently but firmly down on top of me.

She moaned deeply and before the sound had died I had caught the zipper at the back of her dress and tracked it to the end of the line, where the firm round hills of her buttocks rose invitingly. Almost in the same swift motion, I parted the straps of her bra and began to massage the smooth runway of her back. For with women like Myra timing is everything and the first wave of desire must never be allowed to break up on the hard cool rock of reason.

"Don't," she said thickly. "Not now, darling."

"I understand, baby," I murmured. And pulled the dress off her shoulders. It came away with the bra and I kissed the taut pink blossom of one nipple.

"Oh God, God," she whimpered, "why did you make me wait so

long—all these months?"

I was laughing bitterly without sound all the way to the bedroom, carrying her while bending to kiss her, easing her onto the big bed, falling beside her. With deft, urgent fingers she helped me in the impatient release from clothes. And then I was looking down into hungry pleading eyes and the open petals of that moist demanding mouth.

Her warm thighs pressed against me and she groaned, "Now, darling, now! Make up for all the days and nights of wanting and needing you. Make it all up to me, darling."

"I will, baby," I soothed. "I will."

And I did.

CHAPTER THREE

Tarino's house was on a quiet side-street in Miami Shores. The building was shaped like a boomerang, and was a low all-white stucco with a white cupola. It was a giant vanilla sundae, to which, at the last moment, a dash of whipped cream had been added.

There were two cars in the driveway, a Cadillac convertible and a Lincoln sedan. Two others were in the open three-car garage.

Tarino had company.

I jabbed the bell button and immediately the door was opened by a colored maid in a black uniform with a white apron. I gave her my card and told her to tell Mr. Tarino it was mighty damn important for him to see me, and I didn't mean tomorrow. I had really wanted to talk to Kim Rumshaw first. But when I called I couldn't reach her or the aunt, so I figured they might be out somewhere together and I'd try again later. Meanwhile, why waste time?

The maid left the door ajar so I stepped in. If there's anything I hate it's to be left standing outside as if you were some goddamn fund raiser for the garbage collectors' annual wienie roast. And as I walked into the living room the maid was just then opening a door across it, giving me a glimpse of Tarino's den (he probably called it his library) and the backs of four guys seated around his desk under a gray hover of tobacco smoke. For a second, even from the rear, I thought I recognized one of those characters. But then the door closed and the impression faded. The maid reappeared and when she saw me she pulled the door sharply behind her, a frown of disapproval on her face. She fluffed up to me, shaking her head.

"Mr. Tarino, he say for you to wait in the study. This way please, sir."

I followed her to another wing of the house. She ushered me into a room and quickly departed, closing the door behind her.

It was really an office, a small room furnished in dark walnut. It contained heavy pieces with the ornate carving of Italian Renaissance, somber in the tropic setting. An enormous desk dominated one end of the room, an inset bar the other. I found the tiny refrigerator, the glasses and the bourbon. I poured generously over the rocks and sat down with a cigarette. I got right up again because I saw, behind a screen, a bank of green steel files. These were locked, however. Disappointed, I tried the desk. It was also locked and I was reaching in my pocket for something that would give all these locks a hard time when I heard the clunk of a car door. And then another.

I went to the window and parted the drape.

Obliquely I could see the Caddy and the Lincoln. Their lights flared, they moved out of the drive. And I knew that in seconds Tarino would be in the room. So I sat down again, crossed my legs, picked up the drink and waited. Sure enough, in less than a minute, Tarino was standing in the doorway.

His eyes flashed over me, paused at the glass in my hand, returned to my face. I knew he hated my guts for helping myself to his bourbon and it gave me a boot. But nothing showed in his eyes.

"Hey, Rod!" he said. "How goes it, boy? Long time, huh?" He came towards me with his mitt extended. You would think we had been college frat buddies.

"Quite awhile, Eddie," I said. I got up and shook the paw. We both wore identical smiles, gleamingly false, the way dogs grin in the instant before they fang each other from ear to tail.

There was a perfectly comfortable chair opposite me. But Tarino had to go around and sit at the desk. I suppose desks were necessary props in his life which gave him a feeling of command, for he seemed to be always behind one.

I sat quietly in my chair, watching him produce a cigarette case and go through the lighting up routine, stalling while his mind clicked over the possible reasons for my visit.

Tarino wasn't much to look at. He was of medium height with a gaunt triangular face, broad at the forehead, narrowing sharply to point of chin. His eyes were black in deep sockets, his cheeks hollow beneath knobby bones. His lips were contrastingly full and sensual. His arms were too long for his size, his hands too large. He had wide shoulders above a narrow chest. Altogether, about as incongruous an assembly as you could find. But he had a tautness to his body which hinted at scrappy power.

There was strut in all his movements, his manner was bold and cocky. His eyes were full of change, now bright with arrogance, now smoldering with deeply banked resentments.

He sucked on the cigarette, his cheeks collapsing, then exhaled with an insolent purse of his lips. "Yeah," he said again, "it's been a long time, eh, Striker?"

"Sure, Eddie. Not since that shoot-up at your cave on Biscayne. The Frolic. Remember?"

His eyes did a slow fade, his smile flickered like power failure in a storm. "Yeah, I remember. I*s* it my fault if some creep gets drunk and pulls a yard of iron on my boys?"

"Well, no, Eddie. Except that your boys were about to take three yards of padded check out of the guy's wallet. Now if you ran traps that could make a buck without B-girls and sucker tabs for drunks, you wouldn't need a goon squad to keep order."

"All right, all right," he snapped, "that play is over and forgotten. And you're not a cop anymore, remember?"

"Of course, Eddie," I said. "No hard feelings. I was just making conversation."

The heat went out of his eyes and the smile returned. He watched me toy with my glass, jiggling ice.

"You want me to salt that drink up a bit?" he said.

I smiled. "No thanks. If I need a refill I know where to find the bottle."

He swung away from me and put his feet up on a corner of the desk. His black shoes glistened in the light. His black hair had the same shine. He wore a gray flannel suit and a dark blue tie. Conservative. Like any prosperous Madison Avenue executive.

"You didn't come to discuss old times," he said to the wall. "Did you, Striker?"

"Hell no," I said. "There's no profit in old times. I came to tell you just once to leave the Rumshaw girl alone."

His head snapped around, his feet came down from the desk. "What? Say that again, Striker."

"You know, Kim Rumshaw. She wants you to get lost, Tarino. For keeps. And Mrs. Rumshaw hired me to see that the little lady has her way. I told the aunt you and I would have a nice friendly talk and her troubles would be over."

"Is that what you told her?"

"That's what I told her."

"And she believed you?"

"My clients always believe me. Sooner or later."

Tarino smiled. "You make it sound simple. Like an order from the mayor. Well, I'll tell you, Striker, you got guts. Because it isn't simple at all. It's just about as complicated as the law. And according to law, Kim Rumshaw is of age and she can go with anyone, *anyone* she wants to go out with." He leaned back and gave me a frozen smile. A muscle in his jaw twitched. I read in his eyes that this Kim was no minor thing with him. He was ready to shove all his chips on the line. And he had a lot of chips.

"You're right, Tarino," I said. "According to law she can go out with anyone. If she *wants* to. And that's a big if. But she can't be forced."

"No one's forcing her."

"Or intimidated. By threats to her aunt or her boy friend."

"What threats?" His face never changed, his feet went back on the corner of the desk. "I never made any threats."

"Naturally. One of your hoods took care of it."

"I don't hire hoods. You see if you can find a man in my employ who has a record. Go ahead. I'll give you a list of the names."

I got up and walked to the desk. I gave his feet a shove and he damn near fell off his chair. He was sputtering something but I talked him down with a finger in his face.

"Listen," I hissed. "You're not snowing some goddamn social worker sent over by the PTA. Don't give me crap. I know the score from way back. What does it take to hire a couple of mugs no one ever heard of in Miami? Or a dozen? All it takes is dough. And a phone call!"

"All right," he said. His face was crimson. "But don't you lay a hand on me again. You're in my house. Don't try it. I'm no ex-con and I can make a case out of it. I mean it!"

He did. And he was right. I shouldn't have touched him, though I wasn't going to admit it. The smug invincibility with the feet on the desk was a little too much for me. I went back and sat down.

"How long do you think you're going to get away with it, Tarino?" I asked mildly.

"You're just one man, Striker," he said. "The police have been all over this threat business with me and I got a clean bill. Do you expect to make any more of it than they have?"

"The police department," I said, "has many cases. Much more important ones. And a plainclothes cop has about as much routine interest in you and your threats as around a hundred bucks a week salary will buy. That's not very much. Unless someone like me lays the evidence in his lap. See what I mean?"

"What have you got against me, Striker?" he said. "Did I ever get in your way when you were on the force? Did I ever bother you or any friend of yours? Why, for Crissake, I've never been arrested in my life—not even for speeding."

"Look," I said. "I don't give a damn if you run all the gin dives and whore houses in town and beat your old mother on Sunday for kicks. Nothing personal. But if you don't stay away from this Kim Rumshaw babe, I'm going to lose a big fee. Five thousand clams." I smiled. "Be reasonable, Tarino. Lay off, will ya?"

Tarino nodded. He took a file from his pocket and began sawing at a nail. "That's a lotta dough," he said. "It makes sense to go after it. I'd do the same in your shoes, Rod. No kidding." His grin was friendly. "But I'll tell you the truth. This threat business is a mystery to me. Some nut is having a ball at my expense and I've got a couple of guys checking around for answers. But meanwhile, I'm gone for Kim. Way out to hell and gone. And I'm gonna keep ringing her phone and I'm gonna keep traveling around with her just as long as she's willing. The girl says she wants to see me and I believe her. Threats or no threats, that's the way it stands."

He sounded sincere. About the threats. I almost fell for it. Almost.

"That's too bad, Tarino," I said. "I'm sorry we can't get together on this." I stood up. "Just remember, I told you to leave the girl alone. I won't say it again."

"And if I don't leave her alone, what will you do, Striker? I suppose you'll get hard with me. I suppose you'll lay for me some dark night, eh? And then you'll beat me up."

"Not at all," I said. "That wouldn't be legal and I need my license. No, what I'm going to do is to close down your rat traps and send you to jail, Tarino. I could have pulled the rug out a long time ago when I was on the force. But then you were just a nuisance and you weren't really in my department. I still have plenty on you for a start and there are all kinds of ways to get the rest. After which, I know at least two or three guys among the top brass who would be glad to climb higher on your neck. Care to change your mind?"

"No."

"Sorry," I said. "Nothing personal, Tarino. No hard feelings. It's the way I make my living…" I went to the door.

"Okay," said Tarino, smiling, still sawing at the nail. "Just don't get in over your head, Striker. Just don't drown yourself for a lousy five G's. Understand?"

I grinned back at him. "I can swim," I said. "Even under water. And my hide is too tough for sharks. But thanks, I'll be careful." I left the room.

"No hard feelings," he called.

I leaned back in. "Nothing personal," I said. "Because I like you, Tarino. I really do."

CHAPTER FOUR

Kim Rumshaw lived in an apartment building on one of the isles off the MacArthur Causeway. Her aunt had a house on the next isle over—just close enough for Kim to keep in touch with the gold, and far enough for her to nest in privacy.

I guided my Olds over the narrow bridge from the causeway and wheeled right until I found the Flamingo Court Apartments. Of course it was on the water. Almost everyone in Miami who has the loot overlooks the water. Anyway, water is to Miami what sand is to Vegas. The goddamn stuff is everywhere.

It was a little after nine and I knew that Kim would be home. I had just called her for the umteenth time and finally got an answer. She had not been out with aunty, but with the boy friend, Howie. Conditions being as they were with Tarino, this had been done on the sneak—her arrival timed so that she would be on hand in case Tarino rang up for company. Imagine the nerve of that son-of-a-bitch! Apparently his highness seldom called until after nine and the lovers had stolen dinner together. Although from the sound of Kim, the first seven courses had been liquid and a hundred proof. I could hardly blame her.

The Flamingo was the newest and tallest building on the isle. It was all glass and class. The lobby was black and gold, the doorman was at least a general and the elevator boy wore tails. No kidding! He deposited me on the eighth floor and told me that Miss Rumshaw was in apartment E. I found it at the end of a corridor and rang the bell. The door opened. Just as far as a heavy chain would permit.

"Who is it, please?"

"Rod Striker."

"Oh." The chain rattled, the door swung wide.

There are maybe two or three times in your whole life when you will meet a dame who makes your hormones vibrate until your teeth chatter. And when this happens you are at a loss to explain why to your friend Joe Glutz who goes feeble-minded for skinny blondes seven feet tall with short chubby legs and manly chests and wouldn't look at a pint-sized brunette if she stepped on his bare foot with a spike heel. Because a dame is a personal kick and every man to his own sex trap.

But within certain limitations between midget and monster, I have always felt a gal either had it in the gland department or she didn't, regardless of any preconceived package. And this Kim Rumshaw had it! In red neon caps. And I don't mean for love but for lovin'!

Kim Rumshaw was not the sort to make you think of electric blankets. She lived and breathed in an electric field of her own.

She was a quiet-looking little brunette about five-three or four. Quiet as in smoky. The lazy smoke which drifts from the eyes and hints of the blast furnace which produced it. She had straight bangs across her forehead and her long dark hair fell to her shoulders. Simple. No hair acrobatics to take your mind from the face. A small heart of a face, full-fleshed without smudging its gentle contours. The eyes had that gray smoke color with a touch of green, the cheekbones high and smooth, nose tilted, lips flared and curled moistly back at center in a permanent pout.

She was dressed in a low-necked, okra-green sheath which had pink icing here and there and a split skirt so that when she moved you got a large view of thigh and leg encased in charcoal-colored stocking. For the ladies present, she had adorable mammary glands. But just among us male-type men, she had terrific cans, the sweetest goddamn pair of streamlined rockets ever thrust skyward from a female launching pad.

"Come in," she said. "You don't know how glad I am to see you, Mr. Striker."

"My friends call me Rod and my enemies are usually men," I said. "I'm astonished to meet you."

"You're what?" She closed the door.

"Well, your aunt was vague in her description and I never gave Tarino credit for much taste. I'm already beginning to forgive him a little for his determination. We just don't agree on method."

"That man," she said. "That man!"

She moved into the living room and sank onto one of the twin sofas which faced each other across an enormous cocktail table of polished driftwood. The living room must have been something like thirty by twenty, half of it glass. Beyond a wall-to-wall fluff of white rug, sliding doors opened upon a balcony. And before I took a seat on the opposite sofa, I looked down to the splash of headlights along the palm-fingered causeway, the bland dark pool of the bay, the night-face of the city, winking pale neon eyes across the water.

Half a highball sat on the table and she picked it up, crossing her legs with languorous grace, the split skirt flashing thigh and stocking.

"Would you like a drink?" she said. "I've had several and I may have several more. I'm trying to preserve my nerves in alcohol." She smiled easily, but I noticed that her hand trembled as she lifted her glass.

"Sure. I'll have a blast. And thanks."

"I'm drinking bourbon."

"Fine. With water."

She went gliding across the room and returned in a minute with a dark highball. She handed it to me.

"There you are… Rod? Is that what you like to be called?"

"Well, I never had much choice in the matter. It beats the hell out of Rodney. But I owe a lot to that name. It taught me how to fight. I used to clobber the sneer off the face of every little punk who used it."

She chuckled. "You look like a Rod, but not a Rodney. A rod is a gun, isn't it?"

"Yes, and I'm pointed right at you, honey."

Her lips drew back slowly and as she stood looking down at me, she swayed slightly in an alcoholic breeze. Her speech was sometimes halting, but not fuzzy.

"People often seem to be like their names," she said. "Would you take me for a Kim?"

"I would," I said. "Oh, I would!" She was so close I could have pulled her into my lap. And it was a temptation. But suddenly her face closed like a door in a gale. Then her lower lip trembled and her eyes grew moist. She turned abruptly and sat down.

"I don't make a habit of getting stoned," she said. "I think it's disgusting. But I've been under a terrible strain. Honest to God, I've been pulled in so many directions I'm coming apart. I just can't go on like this. Howie, my fiancé, is a little weak sometimes. And you look so un-frightened and…and capable. Do you think you can help us, Rod?"

"That's why I'm here, Kim. I have at least five thousand reasons to give you my best effort. Your aunt is very generous."

"She's a dear. I adore her. Has she paid you the advance?"

"Yes."

"Good. Then we can talk business. How are you going to stop Eddie Tarino? Will you go and see him?"

"I just came from his house."

"You did!" She moistened her lips.

"Yes. We had a lovely chat."

"What did he say?"

"About what I expected. He hasn't made any threats, hasn't or-dered anyone else to, knows nothing of any beating your boy friend got. He's innocent as cambric tea. He'll stand on his legal right to see you whenever and wherever he pleases just as long as you make yourself available. Which, according to him, is just about any hour of the night or day, seven days a week."

"Liar!" she said. "Liar, liar, liar!" She banged her glass down on the table and her eyes could have scorched the walls. "I wouldn't go to a taffy pull with that man if he wore a straitjacket—except that he's practically holding a gun to my head."

"All right. But the fact is he's not holding a gun to your head. He calls up and asks you to trot with him and you go. You're of legal age, no law against it."

She tried to get the cigarette out of her mouth and it caught on her lips. She set it free with a flick of pink tongue.

"What did you expect?" she snapped. "That I would turn him down? So he could send his apes over to beat Howie to death and murder my aunt?"

"No. But you might defy him just enough to make him show his hand."

"We tried that. And the same night Howie was beaten. Next day Aunt Martha was threatened. No thanks. I'm scared to death of him. Did you ever, did you ever in your whole life hear of anything so in-sane as a situation like this? I'm engaged but I can't go out with my fiancé. I'm free and over twenty-one. I've got all the money I need, and still, I'm a slave to a man I despise! Even Russia was never like this."

"Okay, okay. We'll fix Mr. Tarino, one way or another. We'll pull the wheels off his little red wagon. Give me some background to work with. Now, you met him at a party and he asked you to sail away with him on his yacht for the week end. You were engaged but your guy was in Detroit and you said, Sure, Mr. Tarino, why not? Just like that."

"You make it sound rather sordid," she said. "And it wasn't really." She got up and walked to the open doors of the balcony. For a moment she stood looking down, blowing smoke into the night. Then she turned.

"He was so very polite, even formal when he asked me. He said there were going to be at least a dozen other people along, some of them older. And he made it sound as if I would be just another guest, not his date or anything like that. He was extremely casual. A group of his friends going on a little cruise, would I care to come along?

"Well, Howie was gone and to tell the truth I was a little bored anyway. More than that, I had begun to feel just a bit trapped. I was in love with Howie, of course. Madly. But I had met him while I was still in college and since my aunt liked him too and we were going to be married, that was the end of dating. And in a sense, the end of fun. I had always been much too sheltered in the years before, though I was far from a prisoner. But suddenly it seemed to me that all of the excitement of my life was going to die in April when I got married. And I was exactly in that restless frame of mind which made that cruise, and even Eddie Tarino, seem fascinating. So I went."

"And," I said, "once you got aboard, everything was pink lemonade on the fantail. And bridge until beddie-bye."

Her lips curled and she made a kind of sardonic chuckle. "Sure," she said. "Pink lemonade. Hah! Pink panties and strip poker would be more like it. A Roman orgy on the high seas. Oh, the girls were beautiful and perfect ladies. The retiring sort. They retired with the gentlemen in their cabins. I was the only female aboard who wasn't on call around the clock. There was even a rumor you could get your jollies with marijuana, though I never saw any of the stuff. And in between there was gambling. My God, was there ever gambling! I saw enough money lost to pay for that yacht twice over. Then, a couple of hours from home port, you couldn't find a game of jacks.

The roulette wheel, the dice tables, the decks of cards, all of them disappeared. They just vanished."

"I've got the picture, Kim. What about you? And Tarino?"

"Nothing. Just nothing. He never hung around the games or the women. He was almost aloof from it all. He said people would enjoy their little vices one way or another and he frankly made his living providing the opportunity. He seemed so detached from the rest of them. He just talked to me for hours and didn't even make a pass. I found him fascinating. So different from Howie, who is sweet and bright and much better-looking, but more comfortable than he is exciting. Eddie Tarino was just packed inside with violent emotions, all of them showing in his eyes, in a single look. And I was like a little girl at the zoo, sucking a lollipop outside the leopard's cage, deciding to find out what it would be like to squeeze through the bars and pet him for just a second—before she ran."

"But when you tried to run it was too late?"

She hung her head a little. "Yes."

"Because by that time you had slept with him and he didn't want to let you go."

Her head dropped still farther but her eyes looked up and there was the shadow of a smile on her face that I could feel all the way down to the soles of me feet.

"Yes," she said. "By that time I had slept with him."

CHAPTER FIVE

Watching me from the corner of her eye, Kim drifted back to her place on the sofa and tucked her legs beneath her. She sat for several moments in the attitude of that subdued little girl who had found that leopards play for keeps.

"Well," I said "I'm sorry you had to get involved with a guy like Tarino. He runs with a bunch of borderline tramps and you're a taste of champagne after too much beer. The bastard is an egomaniac and he probably thinks you're nuts about him, or would be, if you had the guts to tear loose from aunty and the boy friend. So he's fixing everything in typical gangster style. Later you'll get down on your knees and thank him. That's about the way his crazy mind works."

"Is he really a gangster?" she said in a small voice loaded with awe.

"No," I said. "Not in the old-fashioned tradition. Not with a mob under his command, shooting down members of rival mobs in the streets. In fact, he considers himself as just a shrewd businessman and he wouldn't have anyone around with a record. A diploma from one of the better monkey cages in the country will get you nowhere in today's racket system. This is the era of law-abiding vice with the big wink and the big pay-off. Because there isn't a racket in town that could operate without that payoff. Your modern racketeer plays the gentleman and lives in a swanky house in the suburbs right next to Mr. Morgan Q. Shekels who is president of the bank. He doesn't like violence because it might soil his lovely reputation.

"But there are certain people who can't be bought and we can't allow them to stand in our way, can we? So what do we do? We call in the specialists in murder and mayhem. Maybe they're local, more likely they fly in from Chicago or Detroit or Vegas or some other hood swamp. For a price they'll beat up, knife up or shoot up the opposition, then vanish. Meanwhile, your businessman-racketeer was at his club, surrounded by half a dozen upstanding citizens who will swear he played pinochle until 2 A.M. when they all went over to Judge Take-a-bribe's house for doughnuts and coffee. That's the way characters like Tarino operate. They're slimier than the old style gangsters who never pretended to be anything else."

"My God, the whole thing gives me the creeps," said Kim, finishing her drink in one giant swallow. "How can you fight someone who picks up the phone and orders trouble for you like it came in neat packages shipped by Sears and Roebuck?"

"That's my job, Kim. Let's get on with this. Now, when Tarino put you ashore after that weekend, what was his attitude?"

"Possessive. He acted as if it were just the beginning of a long, cozy relationship. He told me he was crazy about me and he dropped a few hints about marrying me. Imagine! When I told him I was engaged that didn't bother him at all. He seemed to think it was funny, as if it was time for me to put away little boys like Howard Massey and come play with a real man. But he asked a lot of questions, very casually, about Howie and Aunt Martha.

"When he drove me home, he said, 'I'm busy tonight, baby, a business thing. So you'll just have to go it alone. But tomorrow night I'll send someone to bring you over to my club, The Frolic. I'll show you around, check the operation awhile, and then we'll cut out by ourselves. Ten o'clock, and don't be late, baby.'"

"And what did you say to that?"

"I got mad. I climbed out of the car and then I leaned back in and I told him it was a real gay week end and thanks a lot. But I wasn't planning on making a career of him. I was going to be married and I couldn't possibly see him again, even if I wanted to, which I didn't. I told him to take back his heart, I ordered liver. And goodbye!"

"That's when *he* got mad," I said. "And threatened you."

She shook her head. "Not a bit of it He didn't say a word. He just sat there with this lazy, cocksure, how-little-you-know grin on his face. Then he drove off.

"The next night Howie still hadn't come back, though he was due. He had called to say he had been detained. I pictured him having a perfectly marvelous, convention-type ball. And I was irritated. I was in bed, reading a book when the doorbell rang. I threw on a robe and went to see. A man was standing there. He was nicely dressed and very polite. He said, would I please hurry and get ready since it was exactly ten o'clock and Mr. Tarino was expecting me at The

Frolic in just a few minutes. The man said he had a car at the door and he would wait downstairs. He left while I was still trying to explain that I wasn't going."

"But you did go after all."

"Yes. There's something about a man like Tarino who is so absolutely confident, so dominantly male... I don't know, it's intriguing for a time. Because if there's anything I hate it's a spineless slob who doesn't even know what he wants. Anyway, I had nothing better to do. So I went. And I was sorry. Because it was...well, it was a repetition of the first time. I guess every female is wanton in some part of herself. And a certain type man will bring out the worst in her. Eddie Tarino brings out the worst in me. It's a crazy, abandoned feeling and I like it—but not with him. I know I sound confused. But you can loathe someone and be excited by him, too. Regardless, I just got myself in deeper by giving in to him."

"And the next night?"

"Howie was home and I went out with him. It was after he left me that he got the beating. And the threats. And earlier in the evening, some man phoned Aunt Martha and threatened her, too. End of story. Except that Howie and my aunt would like to just ignore the threats and see what happens. They're both very brave. I'm the one who won't let them take a chance."

She jumped up suddenly and took the empty glass from my hand. "Listen," she said. "You've simply got to have another drink with me. Because all this sensible talk is sobering me up by degrees. And if you knew how frightfully nervous I am, you wouldn't allow that to happen, would you?"

"What makes you so nervous?" I said. "Are you expecting Tarino? Relax. I won't let the bad man get you."

Smiling, she roughed my hair. Carrying both glasses, she went off to make with the drinks. Even the touch of her hand had been electric. And I'm not easily electrified.

When she came back, she set the glasses on the table and stood looking down at me. She was frowning, her face drawn with the effort to say something to me.

She sighed and I watched her breasts surge in the tide of her breathing. "I hope," she said, "that you won't get the wrong impression of me. I'm not some little brat spoiled by too much money. I'm quite steady and reliable most of the time. I don't usually have this much to drink. And in spite of what I told you about Eddie…"

"Yes?"

"Well, I wanted to be honest with you because I didn't see how you could help me otherwise. But it was a rather embarrassing admission and I don't want you to think that I'm some…some nymphomaniac or something. Because I'm not."

"You're not?" I made a face like disappointment She tried to ignore it but a smile tugged at the corners of her mouth.

"It's only that Howie was the first man I ever knew in that way and I… I suddenly realized that he might be the last and I got a little panicky. April is only two months off and after I'm married…"

"After you're married, what, Kim?"

"After I'm married it will be too late to wake up to how much I might have missed. Because afterwards I'll never, never have another affair. I wouldn't do that to Howie. Or myself."

"You wouldn't?" I gave her the wide-eyed stare with open mouth. Kidding her because she had been speaking with such pouting, little-girl seriousness.

"No, I wouldn't," she said.

"Well, be calm, honey. April isn't here yet."

"I know," she said. And with that she moved into my arms and fastened herself against me. We touched everywhere, her mouth spreading over mine, her breasts heaving, the impact of that hungry body was such a shock that for a moment I was goddamn near paralyzed. Then I found that split in the skirt and was making use of it when she pushed away and left me. But all she did was to float around the room in a trance, dousing lights. I was still in a little bit of a trance myself.

Then she was standing near in the dark and saying, "Maybe I am a nympho, maybe I am. But I don't care, I don't care!"

And then I heard the zipper. When I looked again, the dress was gone and she was swaying above me in panties and bra. Her hands worked frantically but she couldn't seem to unhook the bra. So she sank down to her knees in front of me and I unhooked it for her. She fell backwards into my arms and my hands wound up under her breasts, lifting while a pale slice of moonlight touched the nipples. She turned half around and I felt one dainty hand creeping over my thigh, dropping down, to squeeze.

"Oh Rod," she said hoarsely, "you are…you are a lot of man!"

She stood, then, naked, but for her panty hose, smiling tauntingly down at me. Suddenly the tease went out of her face and was replaced by a trance-like intentness. Fascinated, my eyes filmed every contour, every peak and valley of her body.

Later, in some idle moment, I would project her on the screen of my mind and the whole goddamn beautiful crazy show would live again.

"Make room for love, lover," she said in a tight husky voice. I pulled her down. She rolled into my arms and glued her mouth to mine. Her hands, like homing pigeons, fluttered to caress me. Then one smooth leg wound itself about mine. She made some artful adjustments and with breathy excitement said, "It's like after the countdown at Canaveral. And now we're rocketing upward, lifting, lifting. Oh Lord, angel-man, don't stop until we come crashing down and… and…"

* * * *

And after a timeless interval of atomic passion, we lay supine, smoking thoughtfully in that vacuum which follows all sensual explosions. Kim had dressed in the dark and was beside me on the couch. She seemed vastly contented and in a playful mood. She turned, pushed a jet of smoke at me, and said, "Say, did you hear the one about the window washer who scared the boss half out of his secretary?"

"No," I answered. "Tell me."

She laughed. And in the little cigarette-puffing hush that followed I heard a small sound, just a whisper of metal. I knew right away but I couldn't seem to move fast enough.

I turned my head and the front door was opening. A guy stood there, a bulky silhouette in the light from the hall. I saw the gun and the arm extending carefully.

I heard Kim catch her breath with a little gasp. She went rigid, trembling against me. I gave her a shove and she went down on the floor, screaming.

The shot came as I hurled myself over the back of the sofa, my weight bringing it crashing down beside me. The gun had a big sound—the thunderous finality of a .45. Kim had stopped screaming and the shot was the only sound, filling the room, bouncing off the walls. Then another. And another.

I had crawled behind the sofa and my own gun was in my fist. I fired blindly, then took aim for the second shot. But I never pulled the trigger.

Because the doorway was empty.

CHAPTER SIX

By the time the cops came, there wasn't anything for them to see but three bullet holes in the sofa. Kim hadn't been hit and that didn't surprise me at all. She was supposed to be plenty scared, which she was. But I had a hunch the shots were fired at me. Why should Tarino have Kim Rumshaw killed? It didn't make sense.

The police offered to leave a man on guard out in the hall. But Kim wanted to stay for the night with her aunt. So I drove her over there and then I went home and paced for a couple of hours—partly because Kim had left me about as relaxed as a Mexican jumping bean, but mostly because I wanted to think out a campaign to nail Tarino for such a long stretch that Kim Rumshaw would be some nice old lady's mother by the time he got out.

One of the things I thought about in that five-mile hike around my living room was how the guy got hold of a key to open that door to Kim's apartment. Because he came in with a key, no doubt about it, and Kim hadn't been loaning her spare to Tarino, even in her weakest moment. Of course to a guy who had stooges like this, a key to most any door was a small problem. But why the hell didn't she think to put the chain on the door? Kim. What she said as an excuse was that since I was there she felt perfectly safe and it hadn't occurred to her. Well listen, baby, let me clue you. Until they send my Superman costume from Hollywood, I'm just as dead from lead as anyone. That's what I told her.

I fell asleep wondering what would happen when Tarino's boy took back the word on what milady wasn't wearing when he burst in and found us on the sofa. That was an unpleasant thought and I must have put it aside quickly. Because what I dreamt about had nothing to do with a jealous and vengeful Tarino…

Around ten the next morning I went to see Kim's boy friend, Howard Massey. His auto barn was out on 79th in the west section. He had a dealership for one of those little foreign bugs. Nice economy but I can't stand the goddamn things because I'm a hell of a big guy and my knees keep rubbing the skin off my ears. I always feel like a gawky oversized kid in a soapbox derby.

Massey Auto Sales was composed of a small showroom and a large lot jammed rump to whisker with the little beetles. These were such tiny jobs you wondered if they gave you a wind up key with the mortgage papers. Behind the showroom was a service garage where they fixed you up with a new spring and rubber-band kit every couple of thousand miles.

I found Howard Massey in a windowless office adjoining the cashier's cage. He was behind an acre of desk, dictating a letter to a redhead of such admirable proportions that I didn't think she'd last a couple of days after the Massey-Rumshaw wedding in April. She gave me a demure glance and departed, leaving me her pre-heated chair. I watched her fanny wave good-bye from the doorway and then turned my attention to Massey.

He was about thirty and close to six feet with a crew cut of reddish brown. He had dark solemn blue eyes and one of those big Kirk Douglas jaws containing a dimple that would swallow a Greek olive.

It was a Florida-type day they don't tell you about in the travel folders—sunless and damn cold for Miami. Over at the beach the sand was frozen so hard the kids were playing hockey. On roller skates! And probably because Massey's office was unheated, he wore wool slacks and a white knitted sweater with a blue diamond design under his open cashmere jacket. All the sweater needed was a two-foot letter across his broad chest to give him the final Joe-college stamp of approval. He would be the sort who took the letter seriously, even now. And I figured him to have a boyishly disarming grin to match sweater and hairdo. He did. He flashed it like a credential as we crushed hands. Then he sat down again and his face returned to a kind of scout master's dignity.

"I heard about last night," he said. "Kim called me early this morning."

His introductory grin had told me that he hadn't heard *all* about last night.

"Hell of a thing," I said. "Close. Another couple of inches and I'd have been coughing up slugs like a skid-row vending machine. But I don't think Miss Rumshaw was ever in any real danger. It was a scare act. When those boys miss, it's because they're not trying."

"That's not the point, Mr. Striker. That's not the point!" Massey pounded a fist the size of a scrub woman's knee into his palm. "She might have been hurt, she might have been killed! You've got to stop this Tarino thug and I don't care how you do it."

"I don't care how, either," I said. "But the law has a rule in the goof book for every occasion. And I guess we'll have to play it their way. Unless I can catch the bastard in the act, I'm gonna sneak underground for enough evidence to keep him dancing in lock step for about twenty years."

"Well, of course I don't want to take the law into my own hands," said Massey righteously. "But I can stand just so much. If I had my way, we'd ignore Tarino. Call his bluff. Then next time he sent one or two of his gorillas, I'd be ready. And I mean ready! I could kill a couple of those guys and sleep like a baby the same night. Scum. That's all they are."

"I take it you weren't quite ready the first time," I said. "When they beat you up."

He frowned, clenched his hands and studied them as if they were a couple of weapons which had failed him like jammed guns.

"There was nothing I could do," he said. "I was completely surprised and it wasn't exactly a fair fight. One of those mugs grabbed me from behind and got me in a strangle hold while the other pounded me. Then they ran off."

I nodded and gave him my thinking-it-over look while I studied him. He was a good-looking guy in a dull sort of way. I mean, you would expect to find his type at the church picnic, helping the old ladies singe the marsh-mallows. Or heading some committee in the crusade against vice and corruption. In war-time, he would be the noble-faced captain who led the company over Sucker Trap Ridge into a goddamn tornado of enemy fire, losing all but three of his bloody men. After, he would have flashed his disarming grin and said he was "just obeying orders." It just never occurred to him to question the orders given by some colonel (as fat on one end as the other) who was sending him into a massacre.

Yeah, Massey was that type and I understood what Kim meant when she said he was comfortable but not very exciting. He was the dream-boy of all the Aunt Marthas.

"What did these guys look like?" I asked him. "The hoods who beat you up."

"I never got a look at the one who grabbed me from behind," he answered. "But he must have been wearing one of those short-sleeved sport shirts. Because I saw his arm and it was tattooed. I couldn't make out the design. The other was about five-nine or ten and burly. He had a hawk nose and his face was pocked. He wore dark trousers and a tan shirt, the army issue variety. That's all I can tell you. There was about half a moon but still it was plenty dark in that parking lot."

"They never tried to hit you in the face—just the body?"

He shook his head. "Just the body. But with inhuman force." He stood up suddenly and hoisted his sweater and shirt, showing me four yards of hair and half a dozen ugly welts on his chest. They had turned purple. "This pock-faced thug gave me the knee down here, too," he said, touching his crotch.

I offered him a sympathetic grunt. "A very professional job, Mr. Massey." He pulled himself into shape and sat down. "Now what was said to you in the way of threats?"

"The one who was hitting me said, 'That's just a sample, buster. Keep away from the Rumshaw doll or next time we'll cut you a new face she won't recognize even after they patch you down at the morgue.' He had a switch-knife in his hand and while he was talking he pressed the point up here under my chin until a couple of drops of blood came. He smeared the blood on my cheek with his finger and said, 'Remember this, sonny.' Then he gave me a kidney punch and when the other let go, he shoved me to the ground. I tried to get up but I was half out and paralyzed for a moment. I heard them run off and then there was the sound of a car gunning, up the block."

"All right. Now, Mr. Massey, during this clobbering you got, was the name Tarino mentioned?"

He examined the ceiling, squinting his eyes and cocking his head as if he was listening to a playback. "No," he said. "I'm certain they didn't mention Tarino. The name wouldn't have registered with me anyhow. Because it wasn't until the next day, when Kim found out that Mrs. Rumshaw was threatened, that she told me about him."

"And what did she tell you?"

"Why, she told me everything!" He wore the smug expression of a guy whose babe has leveled with him all the way down the line.

"Everything?" I said.

"Of course. We have no secrets. She told me how she accepted the invitation to go along on the cruise because she was lonely and Tarino made it sound like there would be a group of older people along as chaperones. And then it turned out to be a gambling ship with wild parties in the staterooms. The minute she saw what an evil mess she had gotten into, Kim asked Tarino to take her back or put her on some island where she could catch a plane. Of course he only laughed. And tried to make love to her. He forced her to kiss him and tore her dress. But she got away and locked herself in her stateroom."

He showed me about a foot of teeth in a proud grin. "You have to hand it to her, Mr. Striker. The kid's got spunk." The smile faded. "But I can't understand where this Tarino gets his gall. I mean, when a girl slams the door in your face like that, what good is she to you even if you can bully her into going out with you? The man is crazy. He's got to be a psycho and he ought to be treated like one!"

Well, after listening to that hearts-and-flowers version of the story she gave him, I damn near laughed in his face. I had to blow the old schnozz and keep the handkerchief over my mouth for half a minute.

Then I got up and I said, "That's about it for now, Mr. Massey. You had a rough time there the other night. And I'm not gonna kid you. Those boys play for keeps. They don't have to bluff. If they come back again they might kill you or they might just cut you into the hospital for about six weeks. And the kind of cutting they do isn't exactly covered by Blue Cross either.

"Now you can take my word on all this because I've had a case or two something like it and I know what I'm talking about. There's a lot of difference between amateur theatrics by some wounded lover and pro-vengeance on order. In one case you got a loud mouth, in the other you got cool bone-breakers and meat-cutters for cash. So play it smart, Mr. Massey. Be careful."

"I'm not afraid," he said with a crooked grin.

"I know. And that's what bothers me. You *should* be afraid." Like I said, this guy was the hero-type.

"Would you let some greasy goon like Tarino intimidate your fiancée?" he wanted to know.

"Listen," I said, "if it was my tootsie, Tarino would know better. Or he'd find out in a hurry. Something would fall on him. Like me.

Or a Mack truck."

"There!" he said. "You see!"

"But I'd try everything else first," I added quickly. "The legal plays. And you'd better, too."

"I have an idea," he said. "A highly legal one. And I think it will stop Mr. Tarino."

"Whatever it is, we ought to discuss it, Mr. Massey. If I'm going to pack this guy up the river in stripes, I have to know what's going on."

He smiled. A kind of wise-guy smile that worried me. "You'll hear all about it," he said. "In good time."

"Okay," I said. "You know where to reach me." I went to the door. "Don't take any wooden coffins." I waved. And went out.

The redhead, the one with the demure face and the saucy behind, sat outside at her desk. Her typewriter was doing about ninety per. She was beating hell out of Massey's letter.

I stood there until the clacking paused and she looked up.

"What a waste of talent," I told her. "I beg your pardon?" she said, demurely.

CHAPTER SEVEN

I goosed the bell button and after too long, Myra Bailey's moist lips spoke to me from the wrong side of the peephole.

"I'm taking a shower," she said.

"So?"

"So go 'way and come back when I'm decent."

"I don't like you that way."

"What way?"

"Decent. That kind I can get at the YW."

"Please, Rod. I'm dripping, you drip!"

"So unlock the goddamn door and run like hell. Don't worry, I'll catch you."

I heard the chain rattle, then the lock flipped. I counted to forty— by twenties—and went in. Myra's classy rump was doing a samba behind a tight twist of towel as she fled from the room. I followed leisurely, stood listening at the bedroom doorway to the muted crash of water. Over the sound, I heard her singing. Not a bad voice. A gal of many talents. And I was getting the use of all but one of them...

I was waiting behind the bathroom door when she came prancing out, naked as a Mexican hairless. Of course she did have the towel. But she was standing with her back to me, drying the front, elbows high. So I reached under her arms and grabbed her breasts, covering the nipples with my palms.

"Guess who?" I said.

It was kind of a dirty trick. But I've know Myra a long time. In certain moods she had a bawdy sense of humor and the subtle approach will only get you more of the Big Tease. I had decided it was about time for direct action.

I was right Because after she stiffened like an over-starched collar in a mangle, she let go a big breath and pressed my hands around her breasts. Then she dropped the towel and turned around, molding against me. My God, I was steamed up and pounding like a flophouse radiator.

She had hold of one of my arms and was pulling it tighter around her, those lips parted and coming closer, as if to gobble me up.

Suddenly her hands tightened on that arm, she spun around, bent double, and sent me flying over her shoulder. I landed so hard on my back I could almost hear the plaster falling in the apartment below. It took me a full aching minute to climb to my feet. I spent the time regaining my respect for the tricks Myra had learned in the L.A. police department.

When I hobbled into the living room, she was sitting in a big chair, wearing a robe and slippers and coolly smoking a cigarette. She wasn't smiling, she hadn't said a word since the tumble. But now she arched one eyebrow into an icy question. Had enough, loverboy? her expression said.

Well, it was funny. I mean, she was so damn casual and undisturbed I had to chuckle. And then she choked back a tiny giggle and I laughed right out loud. We both laughed until we were weeping all over the goddamn room. Then she made a drink and I gave her the latest poop on the Rumshaw case, all business again.

She listened carefully. Occasionally she had a question. When I had finished I got up to leave.

"Well," she said. "What now?"

"You now," I answered.

"Me now?"

"You now, that's right, kiddo. I want you to go down and get yourself a job in one of Tarino's dives. The Frolic."

"What kind of job?"

"Any job. B-girl, kootch dancer, anything! Just so long as Tarino hires you personally. I want that creep to fall all over himself trying to make time with you. Remember, I said—trying!"

"Darling, you didn't have to remind me. Ugh!"

"What're you ughing about, Myra? You've never set eyes on the guy."

"I know the type and I still say—ugh! All right, let's suppose that I get at least a leer out of this bloke. And he hires me. Then what?"

"I can't give you any blueprints, baby. Play it by ear. Just be sure you come back with answers. Some of them could be in black and white—like evidence. Take along mini-tape and record a few items if you like. But for Crissake, be careful!"

I kissed her and this time when she clung to me, she meant it.

"Luck," I said. "Come home safe, baby." Walking away, I heard the door click behind me. And all at once I felt lonesome.

CHAPTER EIGHT

MYRA BAILEY

The minute Rod had gone I felt sort of uneasy. The way I always do just before an assignment. I usually have to work alone and I never know what I'm getting into until. I'm in the middle of it, and then it's too late. Funny—no matter how many times you go out on a case and no matter how many times you come back in one piece, you always get a little nervous just before, as if it was the first caper. Like now with this Tarino character. Then the very second you get into the action, the knots come out and you forget about being scared because you're too busy. When it's over you get the shakes again and you think back and you wonder how you ever pulled it off. But I can be shaking inside like a wet pup and no one will ever know it but me. It's a law I wrote for myself a long time ago. Never show them you're scared!

I went into the bedroom and got a jazzy shade of nail polish from my vanity. The kind you can practically see in the dark. Red as junior's fire truck. I hated the junk. Cheap and gaudy. But I figured Eddie Tarino was out of his element with the Rumshaw dish. Just a new toy, exciting because she gave him the brush after that week end and then his silly ego had to be fed by showing himself he could take any gal he wanted and make her like it. But what the Tarino-types really need down in their grimy little souls is some brass-tongued wench who is so obvious she would stand out like Eleanor Roosevelt in a chorus line at the burlesque.

Of course I could have been wrong about him. And like Rod said, I'd have to play it by ear. But anyway, you don't go looking for a job in a sex trap dressed like the missionary's wife at a meeting of the Women's Christian Temperance Union. So I sat down on the bed and began to put that bright gunk on my nails. Absently, you know. Because I was thinking about something else entirely That Rod! My

God, what a crazy fool. The way he grabbed me and said, 'Guess who?' What an absolute nut! Well, I showed him, guess who. Bet he won't try that again!

What ever am I thinking? Wouldn't that be awful? If he never tried anything again… For a moment there I almost let myself go. When I turned around against him the temptation was unbearable. Just unbearable! But it wouldn't have been worth it. No, I've been that road before with him. He always manages to wall up his emotions and keep at least half an eye for peeling tomatoes, as he calls it. That part doesn't worry me because he won't take any other female seriously. What worries me is that he never quite takes *me* seriously, either. And all the time he seems to be playing just for kicks, I'm lighting a torch for him that would melt the arm off the Statue of Liberty.

No thanks, it isn't worth it. Maybe he'll get tired of that cheap homogenized milk you can find on any doorstep. And then he'll buy the whole cow. I'll be waiting.

Actually, I don't know what it is that makes Rod so damn desirable. It certainly isn't just his looks. He's no Rock Hudson or Warren Beatty. He's got kind of a big nose and his ears stick out a bit. His face is a little too long and that rock jaw… Oh hell, who's perfect if you take them apart feature by feature? The thing is, when you're looking at Rod Striker, you're looking at a man! And I don't mean because he's six-three and muscular and could fight his way out of a concrete mixer. No, it's something inside the guy. You can see it in the eyes. He's all there. A whole man, a kind of harmony of character. Nothing flabby and weak at the core. He's a bad little boy and full of the craziest kind of hell. But not sneaky or grubby. He gets down into the mud but it doesn't stick to him. And you know he wouldn't come apart under pressure, when it counts.

That's Rod, more or less. And if you still don't know what I'm talking about when I say he's a man, forget it. Because I'll need a new language to explain what I mean.

I finished my nails and then I went to the closet and got out a kind of smoky-colored cocktail dress with silver spangles at the bodice. It was a sheath, of course. If you've got a figure and that's what you're selling, don't wrap it in a tent. The dress left nothing to be desired, except a jacket to cover it up so they wouldn't arrest you on the street

Thank God, I had one—a button-up thing which matched.

It took a long time and two pounds more make-up than I generally use, but I was finally ready. I had phoned to find out what time his excellency was expected to arrive at his sewer. A sooty-voiced female told me that Mr. Tarino might be in his office at The Frolic around four-thirty. It was some special business he was attending to and he wouldn't be on tap for more than a half-hour. Time enough....

So at four sharp I called a cab. While I was waiting, I unlocked a drawer of my dresser and took out the snub-nosed .38 revolver and the miniature tape recorder. This tape recorder is a new gadget for police work. Nothing so small has ever been made before. It's not much bigger than an electric razor and it's not as bulky. Flat, you know, and light. I checked it over and then I put it in a secret compartment of the big black suede pocketbook I was going to carry. I have several of these, one for every occasion. They are large but not so gigantic as to be suspicious.

These pocketbooks have two hidden pouches within, one on either side. They are held closed by concealed magnets and can be opened with a flip of the finger. If some sneak gets hold of the bag and looks inside, he sees nothing but the usual face-garbage and the like.

In one of these compartments I placed the mini-tape. Next I wiped off the .38 carefully. You have to keep a gun well oiled in this climate or it will rast. I broke the weapon and inserted some new shells in the chambers. You think of a woman as carrying one of those little toy .25 automatics. But automatics jam and I like a weapon which will stop a muscle-bound ape in stride, even if you don't hit him in some vital spot.

This particular gun is small and has an extremely lightweight frame. Perhaps the lightest ever made. It has one disadvantage. Because of its lack of weight, it kicks like a howling baby. But you get used to it with practice. And you carry death like a feather.

I put the gun in the other pouch with my real identification. The phony stuff was made out under Myra Vanderwalt. If a name is just a bit odd it tends to be more believable. Who would ever believe a name like Bailey? Ha! But you don't take chances in this game. And to go with my fake identification, I even had another address. A cheap little apartment west of Biscayne where I always stayed during any investigation in which there could be danger if I was uncovered. In this apartment I kept some spare clothes and a few minor Vander-walt-type possessions.

As a further precaution, Rod and I were never seen together. Not in Miami. And mostly I worked out of one of the apartments, going to the office only when it was necessary to have a formal interview with some special client.

The last thing I did was to place a call to L.A. I got hold of a Mike Tafuri. He runs a clip-joint called the Tom Cat and he's a friend of sorts. I mean, I can count on him. I gave him certain information. He listened, made a few agreeable grunts and it was done.

I had just hung up and was lighting a cigarette when the doorbell rang. I went down to the cab and ten minutes later I was standing outside The Frolic, measuring myself against the talent pictured in a glass case by the door.

I wasn't worried.

CHAPTER NINE

The Frolic was on Biscayne Boulevard within sliding distance of the docks where the cruise ships tied up, and near Bayfront Park. It was a long stucco building with a lot of wall surface on which was plastered the usual come-on posters—leg-kicking gals in black net stockings with bursting bosoms and man-chewing grins. These were paintings, of course. The real thing could be determined from the photographs in the display case. I knew that once inside, the suckers would be taken by a sex build-up which began with an artless strip routine and ended with B-girls whispering smutty promises at tiny tables in dark corners. The promises would expand in direct proportion to the flow of drinks.

After a while the gal would gulp tea or anything the color of booze, pretending to get as high as the customer. When the guy got his check, if he could still read the total, he would collapse in bleary shock. Or he would come out of his chair fighting. Either way, there would be a plan to handle him. Usually the girl could soothe him with something like, "Forget it, honey. I'll make it up ta ya later. Just as soon as we close. Ya wait f'me, huh, sweetie?"

But if the john really was still waiting at four or five in the morning, she would slip out a back door and steal away.

If you've been in one such joint, you've been in them all. The pattern is much the same. And why the idiots can't see it coming on like a bellhop's palm, I'll never know. But sex is a black velvet curtain, and when it falls before the eyes of the hungry and the lonely ones, the darkness is total.

I pushed the big double doors and went in. For a moment, I had to stand there adjusting my eyes. After the bright sun, it was dusk. A kind of twilight came from windows high over a long bar. There was no other illumination.

Beyond the narrow bar room, stretching to the left, I could see a bandstand and a square of dance floor. A big area jam-packed with a welter of flimsy tables, chairs upended on their surfaces. This was the room of a thousand leers. But since leering is a pastime of the night, the place was in a state of gloomy undress. It had the naked look of tired sin asleep on a rumpled bed.

Surprisingly, the bar was tended by a girl—a slim ash-blonde with features sharp as a broken bottle and pushy little breasts under a red sweater. Evidently business was rushing like rigor mortis at this hour, for the barmaid's only customers were a sailor slumped morosely over his drink, and a beet-haired babe shoving forty and aiming her 45" front at the gob from a dress somewhere down around half-mast.

As I walked past, I heard the sailor drool, "Aw, c'mon, let's blow, Flo. We kin swig better juice'n this in my stall for nothin."

"You talk like a horse," she said. "Nag, nag. Listen, dearie, I'm starved! You buy mamma oats and then we'll think about your little ole stall. Mmmmm?"

I went on down to the other end of the bar and stood waiting between stools. The barmaid moved towards me indifferently, wiping with her towel as she came.

"What'll you have, honey?" she said.

"I'll have Mr. Tarino," I said. "Where'll I find him?"

"You won't," she snapped. "He's not come in yet." Her eyes were battle-gray and slightly crossed. They seemed mad at each other.

"Well, what time does he flap by?" I asked.

"Can't tell," she said. "Any minute, any day. Whyn't ya have a drink while you're waitin? Soon as I see'm, I'll let ya know. So what'll it be? Scotch? How 'bout a champagne cocktail?"

"Calm down, dear," I said. "I don't want a percentage of the joint. I came for a job. Gimme a beer."

She went away and came back with a bottle and a glass.

"Fifty-five," she said.

"Fifty-five! For that I can buy three bottles at the super."

"That'll be fifty-five," she said, palm extended. I gave her the money, counting it laboriously from my change purse.

"What's your name, honey?"

"Sally." Her face was expressionless.

"Well, hiya, Sally. I'm Myra. I'm gonna work here."

"That so? What makes ya so sure?"

"I always get what I go after."

Her gray eyes stopped dueling with each other long enough to climb over me. "Maybe," she said. Her mouth worked once around a chew of gum. "Maybe," she said again. "But I'll be surprised."

"Bet you a beer," I said.

"Bet." She moved off, wiping towards the sailor and his "mamma."

I made the beer last, taking tiny sips. It wasn't difficult. I hate beer. In about ten minutes, Sally came back. Now she moved briskly. She seemed alert.

"He's here," she said. "Mr. Tarino."

"He is? I didn't see him come in."

"You don't know where to watch. There's a side door by his office. Back there. Him and another gentleman, they come in a few minutes ago."

"Bully for them. So what do I do now?"

"You go and see Mr. Tarino in his office."

"Easy as that?"

"I called him on the phone and he said it was okay."

I remembered that she had been talking on a phone which she had pulled from its hiding place beneath the bar.

Sally shook her head. "Funny. I didn't even think he'd see you. Least not now with that other guy—"

"Which way?" I said.

She pointed towards the main room. "You walk to the left and there's a hallway. You follow it until you see a door with Mr. Tarino's name on it."

"Thanks," I said. "Just keep that beer you owe me on ice."

But for a single light, the big strip arena was dark. I picked my way among the tables along the left wall, following it to a narrow passageway. I walked the length of it and found a door marked *Mr. Edward Tarino, Private.* I took off my jacket and draped it over my arm. I smoothed my skirt and then I knocked.

"Come!"

I opened and went in.

It was a good-sized room, longer than it was wide. At one end there was a conference table and half a dozen chairs. Behind this, ebony doors had been parted to reveal a narrow bar with cabinets. There were two long windows of the awning variety and in the distance I could see one of the pier sheds and the stack of a ship.

I knew the man behind the desk was Tarino. He looked about the way Rod had described him in our final briefing session: a large head, high cheekbones, narrow jaw, black insolent eyes. He reminded me a little of Frank Sinatra playing the heavy. He was leaning back in his chair, sitting very still, a cigarette in his hand. Nothing moved but his eyes, little black knives cutting away my clothes with the same clinical disinterest of a surgeon slicing bandages from a patient.

The other man sat in a chair beside the desk, facing me. I had an idea the chair had been turned for my entrance. He was older, just this side of fifty I guessed. He seemed tall and he was slim. He had black hair and a dark brooding face, pale blue eyes with long lashes under heavy brows. He had a sharp nose, a cruel slash of mouth. He chewed half a cigar and wore a perfectly blank expression which managed also to contain as much waiting violence as a cocked gun.

"Who are you?" said Tarino. "Myra Vanderwalt."

"Vanderwalt?" His brows made signals of disdain. "What kind of a name is that?"

"It used to be Garbo," I said, "but I changed it."

"Well don't just stand there, Garbo. Close the door."

"Please?"

He said nothing and I did nothing.

"All right, f'Crissake. Please!"

I closed the door and moved into the room. I wasn't offered a chair so I just stood there, head high, shoulders back. In that dress with my shoulders back a Sultan would have whistled. But they only stared.

"Now," said Tarino, "what is it you want?"

"I dunno. What're you offering?"

"Nothing. I've got a full crew. I'm not hiring any broads right now."

"Then why did you send for me?"

He pulled on his cigarette, pursed his lips and blew smoke at me. "I didn't send for you."

"The girl at the bar, Sally, said you told her to send me in."

"Oh, that." He tossed his feet up on a corner of the desk. "Well, I always take a look, anyway."

I turned around and walked towards the door.

"Wait a minute, miss."

I turned back. "You had your look," I said.

"And you've got a lot of nerve, kiddo." His eyes flashed. "I oughtta throw you out on your can."

"Don't try it, buster," I said.

He glared at me for a moment and I glared back. Then a wisp of smile touched his thick lips. He turned to the other with the cigar. He winked. But Cigar just sat there chewing his stub, ticking away like a bomb.

"What kind of work you lookin for?" said Tarino.

I shrugged. "Most anything. I don't mind hostess if the percentage is good."

"How much experience you got, baby? Where did you sell your bag of tricks before?"

"Place called the Tom Cat out in L. A."

He nodded. As if the name was familiar.

"What've you done here in town?"

"This is my first try. I've only been here a couple of months and I've been taking it easy. I had a fight with my man. He was working at the Tom. So I drifted away. But now the sock is getting a little low. Not much cabbage in the patch, you know?"

"Who runs the Tom Cat, Myra?"

"Fella by the name of Tafuri."

"Yeah," he said. "Mike Tafuri. Will Mike give you a good rep?"

"Sure. The best."

"What did you do for Mike?"

"John con. Salary and percentage."

"Can you dance?"

"I can wiggle. Enough."

"Sing?"

"A little."

He swayed in his chair, hands behind head. "Let's see your legs."

I put the jacket and pocketbook on a table and hiked my short skirt a few inches. I was wearing black stockings. "Higher," he said. I raised the skirt another notch. "Up!" he said.

I gave him a look and then I went on up to the tops of my panty hose.

"C'mon, c'mon," he snapped. "All the way, all the way!"

"I've got just so much leg, you know. If you want a pantie model, trot over to one of those undie factories." I dropped my skirt.

"Bend forward a little," he said. "Give us a bow."

I bent, but I was getting mad.

"Are those real?" he said.

"They were when I put them on this morning."

"Looks like you got a nice pair of knockers," he said. "Pull the dress down and take off the bra."

Tarino had turned to look at the other one, evidently to see if he was enjoying himself. But that one sat like stone, his teeth clamped around the cigar. He looked as if only a corpse would please him.

"C'mon," said Tarino. "You want a job or don't ya?"

Well, I knew it was pretty much what I should have expected. The standard treatment most of the floosies got who hunted that kind of work. But I wasn't going to show myself for these creeps.

"No," I said. "I don't see any point in it Because I don't want to be a stripper. I don't travel that road."

"Figure like that, you could make a mint," said Tarino sadly. "We could pack them in."

"Sorry," I said. "I'll do most anything else."

"You show what you've got or I can't use you," said Tarino.

I picked up my bag and jacket, ready to leave.

Tarino was looking again at Cigar Face. Their eyes met and Tarino shrugged and made an apologetic face which told me everything. He had just been putting on a little show for this guy's benefit. He never intended to hire me.

I went to the door.

"Thanks," I said, "for nothing, you bastard." I turned the knob and was half way out when Cigar spoke for the first time.

"Give her a job, Eddie," he said. "Anything she wants." It sounded like an order. I went back in. "Just like that?" said Tarino.

"No," said the other. "Call up Tafuri. If she checks, anything she wants. This cookie has guts. I like her."

"This gentleman," said Tarino, "is Mr. Markos, Mr. Nick Markos. He owns a big supply house, equipment for bars and restaurants. We do a lot of business, eh, Nick?"

"Yeah," said Nick Markos, rising and removing his cigar. He came towards me. "Glad to know you, young lady. And I'll be seeing you later. Maybe tonight."

He gave me a small pat on the rump and went out. He didn't look back.

CHAPTER TEN

Tarino just stood there for a moment hands on hips, looking after Nick Markos. Then he waved me to a chair and went bounding out the door.

I have learned to take quick advantage of the smallest opportunity, and the second he had gone I was behind his desk. I knew it would be open because there wasn't time for him to lock it, even if the thought occurred to him.

I was right.

I tried the bottom drawer first because that's where you usually find the most interesting items. It contained a green metal box and a .45 automatic. The box was locked and I had to pass it. In the drawer above I found several notebooks. All but one seemed to itemize business expenditures. The last book was some kind of a payroll record. There wasn't time to examine it closely. But I did recognize one name—a detective sergeant in the second district. I made note that his services were worth two hundred a week. A valuable man. I moved on to the top drawer. It held an assortment of junk—pencils and pens, paper, a lighter and cigarettes.

The middle drawer contained a large address book, a banded stack of letters and a telegram. I plucked the wire from the envelope. It had been sent from Chicago.

> LARGE LOT NEW MERCHANDISE ACQUIRED FOR DE-LIVERY OUR CUSTOMERS. SHIPMENT ARRIVING MIAMI MONDAY. WILL JOIN YOU FOR CONFERENCE WEDNES-DAY A.M. MEET TEN-TWENTY FLIGHT 610 EASTERN.
>
> MARKOS

I was memorizing this tidbit when I heard steps in the hall. I jammed the wire back in the envelope and closed it away in the drawer. There wasn't time to make it to a chair so I practically vaulted over the desk. I was leaning against it and investigating something on my leg when Eddie Tarino exploded into the room. I figured the best defense was a distraction and I had the skirt plenty high.

The tight expression on Tarino's face told me he had been worried that I might be snooping in his absence. But when he saw what I was doing his features relaxed and he grinned evilly. I gave him a nasty look and yanked the skirt down. Then I fell into a chair.

He closed the door and flopped behind the desk. For a moment he toyed with the drawers, opening them casually, taking a sly look, closing them. Then he got a cigarette lighted up and swung towards me.

"You're working for me now, Garbo," he said.

"Am I?"

"Yeah, that's right, and don't you forget it! You can cut the wiseguy stuff. I don't take crap from anyone. Not anyone! Understand?"

"Yes, sir."

"You'll do what you're told—no questions. And while you're doin' what you're told, you'll wear a big jackass of a grin the whole time."

I made a huge grimace. "Yes, sir. Yes—sir! But my smile is expensive. What's it worth to you, Mr. Tarino?"

"You'll get fifty per and ten percent of all the drinks you can take the johns for."

"Unh-uh. We went to different schools, Mr. Tarino. I'll take seventy-five and twenty percent."

"No! He shook his head firmly. "Where do you think you are—out in L.A.?. Or Chicago? This is Miami, sister. Fifty and ten."

I got up and slowly gathered my jacket and bag. I went to the door.

"Where you goin'!"

"Sorry," I said. "But I'm not that hard up. There are plenty of other joints in town."

I knew that I had him because this Markos character apparently held aces. And an easy mark is suspicious.

"Be good to your mother," I said, and opened the door.

"Hold it!" he ordered. "Come back in and sit down, Myra. I'll make a call and then we'll see. Maybe we can get together."

I sat down again. Up, down. It was an exercise.

He placed a call to the Tom Cat in L. A. Just as I thought—I could have told him that it was three hours earlier on the coast and Mike would probably be at home. But I let him struggle. He had to place two calls because the first one was station-to-station. It made him mad and I tried not to smile. It was an effort.

While he was waiting he asked me how long I had worked for Tafuri. I told him about five years. Then he wanted to know when I left the Tom Cat. I said it was right around four months ago. These were things I had set up with Mike.

At last he got through to Mike at home. He spoke to him as if they were real buddy-buddy, though probably Tarino wouldn't recognize Mike on the street. There was a bit of shop-talk, very sharp dialogue. Then Tarino checked on my answers. He kept nodding. He finished with some cagey questions which added up to how far he could trust me. While he talked, his eyes slid over to watch me. He was poker-faced and I couldn't tell what was going on in his mind. But when he hung up he gave me a lazy grin and he said,

"You're okay, Myra. You're in. At seventy-five and twenty."

"That's great, Mr. Tarino. When do I start?" I decided it was time now to play it straight. I gave him my all-for-you-boss attitude.

"You're on the payroll as of now, Myra. But I won't put you on the floor tonight. Maybe not for a couple of days. Not until Mr. Markos goes back to Chicago. I want you to help me entertain him."

"Oh? Well, I don't know. I'll miss out on my percentage, Mr. Tarino."

"No you won't, baby. I'll take good care of you. There'll be a couple of bills in it for you."

"That's fine, Mr. Tarino, that's just fine!"

He studied his nails a moment and then looked up slowly with hooded eyes. "I want you to take good care of Mr. Markos, Myra. This man is in a way to do me a bunch of favors. He has some equipment he can sell me at around cost I need that equipment. It's stuff I've got to have for a new place I'm opening. So I want you to do right by this guy. I want you to take good care of him."

"How good, Mr. Tarino?"

"Well, you know, Myra." His smile was cozy as a turned-down bed. "I don't have to tell you what to do."

"Sure, Mr. Tarino. Of course I don't play-for-pay. You might as well know that from the start. But I'll take care of your friend. You can count on it. I'll take care of him good." And not the way you think, Eddie boy, I said without words.

"Thata girl," said Tarino, rising and coming around from behind the desk. "Thata baby!" He reached down and gave my leg a slow massage.

"We'll get along fine," he said.

CHAPTER ELEVEN

Eddie Tarino drove me home in his Cadillac convertible. Home was my grubby little apartment on the west side—Myra Vanderwalt's place.

The apartment is on the ground floor in a pink stucco building which looks as if it had survived a couple of earthquakes and a flood or two—for it lists slightly to port. Tarino followed me down the dark corridor to my door. Hands in his pockets, he moved with a bouncy strut, looking about him with an air of one who takes mental notes for some future purpose.

I unlocked the door and he walked right in behind me. He didn't ask to come in, he just took it as his right. I was already sagging from the strain of the past two hours. It was nearly seven-thirty and I was hungry. In my mind I was gluing myself together for one of the romps in which you pretend to be boiling with a kind of giggly passion while you squirm out of the clinches like a snake with its tail on fire.

But if Eddie Tarino was anxious, it was about something else. He danced into the living room and pulled up short. Feet spread, hands on hips, he took stock of my limp furniture.

"Can't salvage a wreck like this," he said. "We'll have to sink it. Looks like a hurricane sale."

Well, it wasn't half that bad. But Eddie-boy had come a long way since he first gummed a tin spoon.

"It used to be a penthouse," I said. "But it settled a bit."

"Yeah," he said. "But you can't kick too much, it's got wall-to-wall floors."

"I'm sorry you don't like it, Mr. Tarino. I'll have it destroyed in the morning."

He wasn't listening. He had walked across the room to where my phone sat on a table. He got out an address book and scribbled with a pen. Then he bent down and, squinting, he wrote my phone number in the book.

"Would you like a drink?" I asked.

He looked up. "What's that?"

"Well, a drink is a kind of liquid and it comes in a glass and—"

He shook his head, chuckling. "You're a hot one, Myra. You really are. You got a fast mouth. No, I don't want a drink. I'm on the hop."

He stuck his little book in a pocket and went to the door. He glanced at his watch.

"You stay put here," he said. "Keep yourself dressed and ready."

"For what, Mr. Tarino?"

"No questions, remember? Just wait."

"All right, Mr. Tarino."

"And you can call me Eddie. Except around the help. That mister stuff sounds like a rib the way you say it."

"I didn't want it to sound like that, Eddie. I meant every word of it."

"It takes a broad like you to get away with certain things and come out with a full head of teeth. You're all right, Myra. But take it easy with Mr. Markos. Play him straight and careful. I won't stand for any foul-ups."

His lips tightened and his eyes took on a menacing glint. I knew he was dead serious and for some reason I couldn't understand, I was touched with a pang of fear. I realized that all my little cracks and barbs were part of a brave front. Underneath I was just a little scared.

"Don't worry, Eddie," I told him. "With velvet gloves."

He looked at me solemnly for a moment. Then he turned and walked off.

As soon as he had gone, I called one of those chicken-in-the-basket places and had them send up a big order. When it came I covered myself with an old bath towel. I didn't want to get any spots on the gown because I had the impression Tarino liked it and didn't want me to change.

Finished, I felt better. But I hate to eat alone and suddenly I needed the reassuring sound of Rod Striker's voice. I went to the phone and dialed him. I didn't get an answer so on an off-chance I phoned the office. Nothing there, either. He was probably out working some angle of the case. Night is just the other face of a job which has no hours and never stops until the pay-off. And then the next assignment begins.

I felt cast adrift and there was in me a woman-hunger for some kind of permanent affection and security. At that particular moment I would have traded all of my so-called excitements for the dullest routine of a housewife.

I was able to make myself a drink because I always keep a small supply in that apartment. I carried the glass and a book to a chair and sat down. I read two pages and couldn't get into the story. Whenever there is time to read, my mind seems to be a jungle with problems stalking me from some dark foliage of my subconscious. Eddie Tarino was creeping up on me so I closed the book and took another look at him.

In a sense, I could understand why the Kim Rumshawtype would be drawn to the fire which burned in him, even if only to leap back quickly from the flames. Eddie had that basic, naked animality which does not cringe behind the flimsy wall of social hypocrisy. His eyes said to a woman— Come out from hiding there in your silky cave. I know you, baby, and what you are. An animal, just like me. I see behind your coy smiles and poses. I see you to the core. And I am not afraid of you or what you might think of my nakedness, for I see you naked, too. So come out and play and I will show you passion stripped of pretense, lust without fear.

You see, by all her training, a woman is afraid to reveal herself. And since training argues with hidden desire, the total animal like Tarino can sometimes challenge a woman into bed by lending her his own animal courage.

If that's not clear, it's still a fact for many women. And the result is a kind of hypnotism from which a woman soon awakens once returned to her environment.

That seemed about the way Kim got involved with Eddie Tarino. And when he wouldn't let her go, the trouble began. It could have been a rather minor trouble for him. He could have escaped with a shrug. But he was stubborn and full of his ego, and his hunger was out of control. And what began as a small thing would swallow him altogether. Because his method of intimidation was sly and he couldn't be caught by the front door. In order to stop him now, we had to uncover all the other evils surrounding him. We had to bring down the whole house because the trouble was hiding underneath.

It has always interested me that some little quirk of character will trip the mightiest Hitlers.

Anyway, I grew weary of my amateur head-shrinking and tried the book again. I made it through half a dozenChapters and the doorbell rang. It rang twice before I had taken a last look in the full-length mirror behind the bathroom door and gone to answer it, expecting Tarino.

But Mr. Markos stood there gazing at me with that perfectly blank, cocked-gun expression.

I've been dealing with this hard old world in a hard way for a long time. But I've never met a man in my whole life who made me so downright uneasy as he did. There was no smart answer for this one. I couldn't find a key to open him up.

You're afraid of him, a voice whispered. And all the time I was shouting the voice down, I knew it was true. "Evening, Mr. Markos," I said. "Won't you come in?"

CHAPTER TWELVE

Something touched Markos' face which might have passed for a smile. He stepped into the living room with long slow strides. He was wearing a dark blue suit with white shirt and gray silk tie. He carried a gray felt hat with a high crown. Since hats in Florida are practically a curiosity, it seemed odd. But according to the telegram in Tarino's desk, Markos had just arrived that morning from Chicago and I suppose coming from that ten-degree weather with snow on the ground, it was difficult for him to imagine going anywhere without a hat. Anyway, Markos was not a man to be kidded about his hat—or anything else.

He stood in the center of the living room, turning the hat slowly in his hands and looking around him with the slightly puzzled attitude of one who wonders why he is there in the first place.

"Very nice," he said, making it sound like an accusation. Then he turned and walked out the door, adjusting the hat carefully to his head as he went.

There was nothing for me to do but grab my pocketbook and follow.

I found him waiting for me at the curb, standing beside a gray Lincoln sedan. He had the rear door open and for a moment *I* wondered if I was to sit in back while he drove. But then I noticed two men on the front seat. I climbed in and their heads turned just an inch or so towards me and I got a better look at them.

The driver was one of those young-old types. He had what the slick magazine writers call handsome-clean-cut-features-with-a-clean-cut-jaw. He was also clean-shaven. He was the sort of junior executive material which leers down at you from enormous billboards. But his mouth and especially his eyes were positively ancient. Hard and old as sin, as they say.

The other was a Latin with mocha skin and the inevitable dark hair and thin mustache. He was below fifty but otherwise I couldn't have guessed his age. He was chunky. Beside the driver he seemed short. His eyes were small and bright in a puffy face with a receding jaw.

Markos sank down beside me and closed the door. He didn't introduce me to the others and not a word was spoken. We pushed off into the night traffic, gliding west for a block and then turning south. Markos stared blankly out the window while the two in front peered straight ahead. The silence was oppressive and even ominous.

I had the unreasonable conviction that something had gone wrong since I last saw Tarino; that I had been forced out and now I was being taken towards whatever vengeance was planned for me. It was one of the few times in my life when I couldn't think of anything to say that wouldn't sound idiotic. But I had to hear my own brave little voice.

"A beautiful night," I said.

Markos turned slowly and gave me this cool stare. A rebuke. The kind you would expect if you had desecrated the silence after a funeral oration with some stupid pleasantry. He returned his gaze to the window. Traffic droned past rhythmically. There was the grunt and throb of a trailer-truck changing gears; the long cone of a raised headlight examined Markos' brooding features and winked out.

"It was so cold yesterday," I said. "Not like—" (I almost named Chicago) "not like the rest of the country, of course. But you know," (with a chuckle) "pretty frosty for us."

Markos, in the middle of lighting a cigarette, nodded.

The hand with the cigarette came to rest on his knee, the cigarette glowing skyward between pale fingers and becoming a tiny beacon in the dark.

"But then today," I hurried on, "all of a sudden it warms up and we're in the seventies. That's the way it goes… I see you're wearing a hat, Mr. Markos, so you must come from a pretty cold climate. Well, that's no brainy deduction, is it? But what I mean to say is that this must be such a marvelous change for you—this balmy weather. Do you come down here very often…? No? Well, I suppose the first time is really the best, don't you think?"

Silence.

"By the way, Mr. Markos, where's Eddie? Mr. Tarino."

"Myra…" Markos raised a long finger and aimed it casually towards my face.

"Yes, Mr. Markos?"

"Myra, you talk too much. Why don't you shut up, like a good girl." He spoke softly, almost soothingly, but his little smile was the blade of a knife. "Just shut up, that's all."

"Sorry, Mr. Markos," I said, and despised myself for that meek whimper of an apology.

Markos settled back in his seat. His face closed altogether and again he stared from the window.

We turned a corner and slid west again. This was a narrow street of wood-frame houses, antique eyesores, peeling and overcome by untamed vegetation. The city fathers must have decided it was not a street that could withstand illumination and, except for an occasional eye of jaundiced light, darkness was complete.

After a time we came into an area of squat buildings which looked as if they might house some minor manufacturing plants. And a block beyond these we pulled up before a long cement building with two tiny windows high up near the roof. From these windows came a feeble hope of light.

The place had only one door that I could see. And this was a big steel corrugated affair, large enough to admit a truck. In black letters on the white surface there was the identification:

MARKOS SUPPLY CO.
Equipment and Supplies for—
Hotels * Restaurants * Bars

I assumed that this was a warehouse, and that later proved to be correct.

The driver turned around to look questioningly at Markos who said, "Well, Remick, what're you waiting for?"

Whereupon the one called Remick opened the door and got out. He was one big hunk of man, bigger than I had thought. He stood by the car waiting and staring in at me. The Latin was turned in his seat, watching with his fierce demanding little eyes.

There were a few beats of silence during which Markos worked his jaw and eyed the Latin. I was extremely nervous but tautly ready. I had opened my pocketbook, taking a cigarette from the pack within and holding it ready for the lighter I pretended to hunt in the bag. Actually, I had opened the gun compartment and my hand was clasped around the butt, finger on the trigger. The gun wasn't too comforting. There were three of them and probably they were all armed.

"All right," said Markos to the Latin. "This is it."

I had the gun half-out. But then he went on, "I'm sure you'll find the equipment satisfactory, Carga. My boys are going over it now and we should be able to make delivery to your hotel in a few days. If you're happy, we'll discuss the terms later, eh?"

"Yes," said Carga. "But you know I am in a hurry." His teeth flashed in the dark, he spoke with a small, lisping accent. "I must have the kitchen equipment immediately. Yes, especially the equipment for the kitchen."

"I know, I know," said Markos with his knife-smile. "Why do you think I brought you down here at this hour of the night? It's a favor. We conduct our business in the daytime."

"Very well," said Carga. "Later, then." He climbed out and shut the door, moving off with the one called Remick. At which point I heaved a mental sigh which, if real, could have been heard a block away. I let the .38 fall back into the pouch.

Markos watched the two until they had reached the door and passed inside after a wait in which they must have pressed a signal button. The door rolled upward only a few feet and they had to duck under. Then the quick splash of light was gone and Markos got out. He eased behind the wheel and beckoned for me to come up front.

We turned around in a driveway and gunned back down the street. Markos said nothing until we had reached a main thoroughfare and had swung towards the ocean. Then his hand dropped lightly on my knee and squeezed.

"Now," he said. "An end to business." His voice and manner had changed in some subtle way. "We'll have a little party at my hotel. Champagne and a nice spread—the works. How about it?" He braked at a light.

"Fine, Mr. Markos. I'd like that. Who's going to be there?"

"Does it take more than two for a party?" He laughed, a metallic rasping.

The light flicked green and he stepped down hard on the gas.

CHAPTER THIRTEEN

Markos was staying at a hotel on Miami Beach, one of those colossal dreams of stone and glass which can be found in few other sections of the country.

We pulled up to the door and a parking attendant took the Lincoln. But not before Markos had opened the trunk and removed a brief case. I made special note of that case because I had an idea it was going to interest me.

In the vast lobby with its fountain behind glass and its tile mosaics, Markos sought the bell captain and gave him a list of items to be sent to the room.

"How soon do you want this delivered, sir?" said the captain.

"Ten minutes ago," said Markos. And gave him a ten-dollar bill which he peeled from a roll that would embarrass a bookie.

We stepped into an elevator and climbed until I thought we must have run out of floors, riding into space the way they do in those animated cartoons. Then we walked down a hall of mauve carpets and up a few steps to a vermilion door with a small gold crown in bas-relief. There wasn't another door like it on the floor.

Markos produced a key and we entered an enormous living room done lavishly in Chinese modern and practically ringed with floor-to-ceiling glass. In one corner of the room there was even an ebony grand piano.

"Penthouse," Markos announced. "Nothing to beat it in the whole goddamn town. You like it?"

"It's gorgeous," I said, and it was.

"Bill and a half a day," said Markos. "C'mon, I'll show you the layout."

There were two great bedrooms, each aimed at the sea, one of them containing a king-sized bed. In this room Markos placed his gray felt hat on top of a dresser and tucked the brief case in one of its drawers.

The rest was a small kitchen and a dressing room set with mirrors. There were two baths. A walled balcony encompassed the entire apartment, although the balcony was sectioned so that each room had a separate area.

Markos took me to the section which fronted the living room and we stood there looking out and down upon the glazed multicolor of lights west and the giant formless shadow of the ocean east. Directly below was the cement court with its scatter of tables, a tiny bar beside an Olympic-sized swimming pool. The pool was lighted and the water had a look of azure purity. Even at this hour a few late swimmers splashed and dived.

Markos bent his head and said, "It's along ways down, eh?"

He said so little. And somehow when he did speak, the simplest statement seemed to carry undercurrents of meaning. So I looked at him from the corner of my eye, but there was nothing in his face. He simply stared below.

I followed his gaze down the long sweep of the building to the far distant pavement. I am not overly afraid of height. But at times it has an odd effect upon me. I feel as if the ground has a magnetism which attracts me towards it in some insidious way. This was one of those times and there was a rushing in my ears, a hollowing in the pit of my stomach that made me weak with the light-headed dizziness of too much wine. I turned away.

"It's a lovely view," I said.

He studied me for a moment. I had the impression that he had discovered my little fear just then as I peered down. It was an unsmiling look he gave me, yet smiling just the same. His eyes roved over my body.

"I liked the dress better this afternoon," he said. "Without the jacket." It was a command. "Well, it's a little cool tonight," I parried. "Take it off," he said.

I removed the jacket and folded it over my arm. His jaw worked, his eyes probed my breasts.

"I want to thank you, Mr. Markos. For getting me that job this afternoon."

"You will, baby," he said. "You'll thank me."

And then he reached a big arm around me and pulled me against him. His hard thin mouth came towards me and I wanted to turn my head but didn't dare. There was the foul stench of spent cigars. And quickly his lips fastened on mine like a clamp of moist metal.

I closed my eyes and made a small pretense of enjoying it. There was nothing in my mind but a single object—the long tube of toothpaste which sat on a shelf of my medicine cabinet. I saw it so plainly I could almost read the brand.

At last his mouth came away. But then his hand stroked my bare shoulder and slithered down to the top rim of my dress. His hard fingers went beneath and clutched the material. He was going to rip it away, I could see it in his eyes. I was about to grab that hand when he let go and turning about sharply, moved into the living room.

I spent a minute just gulping air, then went inside. He was gone.

I tried to think what to do. He was unpredictable. I had no guide to what made him tick. I had to keep him happy. Somehow. Just long enough. Really stalling, I went into the dressing room and repaired the damage to my make-up. I was just finishing when I felt his presence.

He was standing in the doorway, leaning on the jamb. He had removed his coat and tie and his shirt was unbuttoned almost to the waist.

"Hello," I said.

He didn't answer. He made a tiny beckoning movement with his head. And again he was gone.

He wasn't in the living room or on the balcony. So I knew exactly where he was. And now I could think of just two choices—go there, or run from the apartment and keep on running. I compromised. I would go to him and somehow I would talk him back into the living room.

He was lying on that big bed, feet crossed, a pillow behind his head. I stood waiting in the doorway, caught by the very stillness of him, especially his eyes. I thought how absurd it was to imagine I could talk him anywhere. What would you say to a man like him?

His eyes ordered me to come in. They spoke obscenely and with hypnotic demanding—the way snakes are said to fascinate. And before I understood why, I moved towards him.

"Close the door," he said. I closed it.

He grabbed me the minute I was within reach and pulled me down on top of him.

"Now," he said. "I'm gonna chew you up, baby. And when I spit you out, you'll know you've had a man!"

My mind raced, scurrying frantically for an idea that wouldn't destroy all I had gained. His arms were steel bands closing around me. I knew how to injure him so he would let go. But that would be the end of it and—

And then there was a distant pounding on the hall door, growing louder. I felt him go limp, listening.

"Goddamn," he said. "Goddamn, goddamn!"

He shoved me away and buttoning himself, left the room. I went right out behind him. He had the door open and two bellhops were wheeling in carts of food and champagne.

Thank God, thank God!

CHAPTER FOURTEEN

When the bellhops had gone I looked at the handsome spread of cold cuts on the table and the iced buckets with their bottles of champagne. And I said, "Six bottles, Mr. Markos? That's a lot of champagne." My God, this was going to be a night!

He was taking the cork from one of the bottles with a lot of wrenching and pulling and he didn't look up. "Ever hear about the babe who took a bath in champagne?" he asked.

"No."

"She fizzled to death." He laughed and I made a sound like laughter. "Just fizzled out," he said with a final chuckle. The cork popped and he poured into glasses, passing me one. He lifted his own. "Just be sure you don't fizzle out on me, Myra." We drank.

Then the phone rang. He frowned, moved across the room to answer it.

"Yeah?… Well goddamnit, you're early! I told you not to come until—" He looked at his watch. "Yeah, you're right. It's eleven. Okay, come ahead." He hung up.

"We're gonna have a little company," he said. "But don't let it bother you, they won't stay all night."

That certainly was reassuring.

He went into the bedroom and came out fully dressed. He was pouring more champagne when there was a knock on the door.

"Answer it," he ordered.

I went to the door and it was Eddie Tarino. There was a young girl on his arm and I knew from Rod's description it must be Kim Rumshaw. A quiet face with a loud body. I mean, it shouted sex. She was dressed in a pale blue sleeveless sheath and she wore a mink stole.

Eddie introduced us and I was sure she didn't have an inkling as to who I really was, especially since the name Vanderwalt was unknown to her. She smiled quite pleasantly, giving me the quick study, the way females automatically measure the competition. If she was under any strain, if she was frightened or intimidated, it didn't show. She appeared to be perfectly poised. In fact, she was gay and there was an air of dominance about her.

I was puzzled.

Eddie hustled Kim up to Markos and made the introduction, calling him "Mister Markos" as always, and with much respect. Whatever impression she made on Markos, he gave her only a curt little nod and a glass of champagne. He gestured towards the food. In the world of Nick Markos there were apparently just two kinds of people—those he tolerated and those he did not. God help the latter.

Among other things in that tower, there was a radio. The lights (with the help of Tarino) were cut to one, and we danced. Markos was a lousy dancer. He knew certain steps but he was stiff. I suppose in his own peculiar way he was too dignified and too unbending for anything which required such a loose obedience to rhythm.

He was also unable to have a good time. He went through the same motions of drinking, eating, dancing (he never grew more talkative) but he just wasn't quite there. He wasn't with it, as they say. If anything, he drank more than we did. But whatever emotions alcohol fired in him, he simply became more and more brooding. He was smoldering inside and you couldn't even see the smoke.

That bothered me. He was a kind of nut. And what do you do with a nut if you can't crack it?

Meanwhile, Tarino and Kim were oblivious. They were both getting high, thoroughly enjoying themselves. So it seemed. They were drinking and laughing it up and dancing around the room, Kim with her shoes off. I could see that Tarino was getting amorous. He was whispering suggestions with a sly look on his face. She wasn't saying no and she wasn't saying yes. She was laughing. Not with him, but at him.

Tarino didn't get it—that he was being laughed at. Not at first. But the drinks were making him ten feet tall and he was becoming insistent. And just as insistently, she was laughing him off. An arrogant laughter, needling and superior. In effect, she said— *You poor boob, you unknowing slob.*

I was sitting next to Markos on the sofa, drinking and watching, with great interest, because I knew something was going to give. Markos was silent, morose. He hadn't touched me—not a pass. It was as if he was so sure of me he didn't have to bother with any games. When the time came he would simply take me and that was that. Meanwhile, he was above any public charades.

Tarino had maneuvered Kim to the hall which led to the bedrooms. He had danced her over there. He said something. She laughed. He stopped dead, got hold of her arm and began to guide her away, none too gently.

"No!" she said sharply. "Not now, not tonight, not ever!" She spoke loudly, her voice cutting through the music.

I looked at Markos. He showed no interest. He was a zombie.

Tarino was furious. He knew that we had heard. He grabbed her arm again.

"Wait!" she cried, wrestling free. "I want to show you something."

She flounced across the room and came back with her pocketbook. She opened it and produced a white folded piece of paper. She pressed it into Tarino's hand. "There—you bastard," she said. "That'll hold you!"

"Who you talkin' to!" screamed Tarino. "And what the hell is this?"

"Read it, read it!"

He gave her a look, then marched to the one light and opened the paper. He read it. Something electric came over him and he read it again, glaring up at her, then down at the paper. He moved towards her and gave her a giant slap across the face. She fell. I started to get up but Markos put his big hand flat against my stomach and shoved me back.

"You think this'll do you any good?" Tarino hissed down at her. "You think so? Just wait 'n see, baby. Just you wait 'n see!"

He tore the paper in half. And again. He dropped the pieces on her face. Then he leaned down and picked her up in his arms, her tiny fists smashing at him. He carried her struggling into the other room. A door slammed.

"Aren't you going to stop him?" I asked Markos.

"Mind your own business," he said. He got up and poured himself another glass of champagne. He must have had more than a dozen. He didn't even stagger.

I went over and picked up the fallen pieces of paper. I spread them on the table under the light and puzzled them into the right order. Then I read.

It was the photostat of a marriage license. As of yesterday, she had become Mrs. Howard Massey.

CHAPTER FIFTEEN

It wasn't more than five minutes later that there was still another knock on the door. This time it was the Latin, Carga, and the big young-old one called Remick. Markos gave them a drink and then he went to get Tarino. There was going to be a meeting. I gathered this from the conversation. Now Markos was all business.

Kim came out of the bedroom with red eyes and a puffy face. Gone was her bravado. She looked thoroughly cowed, frightened. Tarino hurried her to the door and came back without her.

"You'll stay," Markos told me. "You'll wait in the bedroom." He turned off the radio and then he went over to the one called Remick and took him aside. The other two were guzzling champagne. They had their backs to me. And in that moment I slipped the recorder from my pocket and flipped the switch to "record." Quickly I placed the little box under the sofa, well out of sight.

I had barely settled back with a cigarette when Markos came and led me to his bedroom.

"Wait here," he said. "You and I got some unfinished business. Right, baby?"

I tried to smile.

He closed the door.

I sat down on the edge of the bed. Thinking furiously, I finished the cigarette and mashed it in a tray. I got up and went to the door. I placed my ear against it and listened. I couldn't hear a murmur. Cautiously, I opened the door.

Remick was standing just in front of it. He turned.

"Back, sister," he said. He gave me a thin leering smile as his eyes swarmed over me. For a moment I thought he was coming in. He had that look. I closed the door.

Well, I was a prisoner. That was obvious. Probably Remick was there to see I didn't get close enough to listen. But I was still a prisoner. And I was worried. These guys took what they wanted, any way they could get it. Just to be around them, to be exposed innocently like Kim, was dangerous. But to spy on them, if you got caught, was suicide.

Still, the job had to be done, and I had long ago accepted the risks.

I had one advantage. Time. My guess was that I could figure on at least a half-hour. Five minutes should be plenty.

I went to the door and quietly pressed the lock button.

On the dresser there were two tiny lamps. One of them was lighted, otherwise the room was dark. Softly I pulled the bottom drawer open and removed the brief case. There was a zipper and I slid it back.

In one compartment there were banded stocks of money—hundred-dollar bills. The other contained some ruled sheets of paper. I didn't spend much time with the money. I was interested in those papers. I plucked them out and began to read.

It was some kind of inventory.

BARs — 26 cases — 20 pc
TMGs — 43 cases — 35 pc
GRs — 71 cases — 40 pc

There were many other listings. I didn't understand any of them. On the surface they looked harmless enough. But every instinct told me there was something vastly illegal here if you could decipher it.

I was turning to the second page when a terrifying awareness crept over me. I was being watched. There was a presence in the room. I felt it, I knew it! Yet, it was impossible…

There was a mirror over the dresser and without raising my head, I took one fleeting look.

Nick Markos stood frozen in the doorway to the balcony. Somehow he must have climbed that walled partition which divided one section from another, coming catlike into the room. First he must have tried the door. And when he found it locked…

As ever, his face was a blank. But his eyes were hooded and he was positively coiled in that doorway. The tension was almost visible, an electric force reaching out from him.

My pocketbook with the gun was out of reach on the bed. And I knew that if I didn't think of something I would never leave that room alive.

My back was to him, the papers held in close to my body. I was sure he couldn't see exactly what I was doing and didn't know I had caught his reflection in the mirror. With one hand I sneaked the papers into the case, while with the other, I removed a wad of bills. I did this without changing my position a fraction. Now I leaned forward to the light and made a show of examining the hundreds. My point was to convince him that my only interest was in the money. It might give me a small chance.

After a moment or two I took a single hundred-dollar bill and returned the rest of the stack to the case. I zipped it and put it away in the drawer. I turned with the folded bill in my hand, moving towards my pocketbook. If I could get that bill inside and reach the gun…

But he was on top of me. One hand grabbed my hair and pulled my head back viciously, the other clamped over my wrist as my fingers touched the bag. He snatched the bill and then his big fist smashed against my jaw. For an instant I felt myself flying backwards. But before I touched the floor, I was unconscious.

When I came to, I had the impression that not much more than a minute had passed. In an odd way it seemed darker. A breeze touched my face. My jaw ached and I felt light-headed. Cool cement was beneath my body, yet for some reason I pressed lightly against it, weightless. My arms were stretched back over my head, also weightless. My eyes focused—on nothing. Space.

I felt strangely uncomfortable. Pulled taut at both ends. My ankles seemed clamped by circles of hard metal. My legs were cold.

I lifted my head slowly and looked. My skirt was around my hips, my legs bare. Above me, far above me, Markos looked down. He was smiling. No, he was laughing in a nearly soundless way. His hands were clenched around my ankles, biting my flesh with their hard grip. I couldn't understand why he was holding my legs up.

And then I saw that he was leaning over a wall. And I turned my head and looked down.

I saw the pool—empty now, but still lighted. And the little bar, and the court with its scattering of tables—toy tables, little mushrooms sprouting up at me. Directly below, an enormous distance down the white face of the wall, there was a vague section of pavement which shimmered and beckoned.

I grew dizzy. Fear spread through me like a quick violent poison.

I was paralyzed.

"I've been waiting," said Markos, sounding a long way off. "It's no fun if you don't see it happen. Ready, Myra?"

I tried to speak and couldn't. I tried to scream and nothing came. I curled upwards toward him, grasping air, falling back again. He let go of one leg and I dangled, swaying in space.

And then, finally—I screamed.

CHAPTER SIXTEEN

I was a rag doll, limbs askew, dangling hundreds of feet above the earth. It went on and on. For what seemed an eternity. Then he pulled me up a ways, caught my other foot and hoisted me back over the wall. I collapsed against it, sobbing for breath. The stone floor beneath my feet felt unreal, impermanent. My eyes were bugged out of my head with fear, my legs sagged and trembled.

Hands on hips, Markos stood watching me as if I was some writhing specimen under glass. His little smile said he was thoroughly enjoying himself.

"You think I was afraid to let you go?" he asked. "You think I chickened out? It would've been easy. No problem. You got drunk and fell over. Or you knocked yourself off. Who knows? We're in the other room minding our own business. We hear a scream. We rush in. We look down. There you are, so much rhubarb oozing all over the cement. That's my story. Three guys back me up. The cops write in their little books. Suicide. And then they beat it, shaking their heads. Easy."

"You're crazy," I said. I took a deep, shuddering breath. "Out of your mind. A hundred dollars, just a hundred."

"You think I care about the lousy hundred bucks?" He stepped closer, squinting into my face. "But no one crosses me and gets away with it. Not for a hundred. Not for fifty. Not for a nickel! Understand?"

I could only nod.

His hand went around my throat, his thumb caressed my windpipe.

"I don't read you, baby," he said. "Not yet But I'm gonna. I'm gonna open you up like a clock and see why you go off like a bell in my head. You're too smart to swipe a hundred bucks from a guy like me. You'd figure the odds, you'd know you wouldn't get away with it. You've got an angle and I'm gonna find it. If it's only that hundred bucks, you got nothin' to be afraid of. You just now learned a lesson you won't forget. But if it's something else, if my hunch is right, you better take that big jump over the wall. Before I get back."

He turned and went into the room. I saw him pick up the brief case. Carrying it under his arm, he went out.

Never for a moment had it occurred to me that he might return for that brief case. But that's just what happened. He must have needed those figures, the inventory, for the meeting. Well, you can't win them all. There are things you can't possibly foresee. And it's those things which can kill you.

I went into the room and found a cigarette in my bag. I watched my hand shake trying to light it. I inhaled deeply, exhaled on a long sigh. My God, my God, what a night! And it wasn't over. It could be just the beginning. A guy like Markos smells smoke and you can bet he's going to find the fire. The hard way. For me.

I had to get out of there. No way out but down and I had to escape!

I looked at my watch. Not more than five minutes had passed since he caught me. But a single minute suspended in space is forever. Yes, I had to get out of there. And what's more, that recorder, our mechanical ears, had to go with me.

There was a phone on the night table. I stared at it. I picked up the receiver.

"Operator." A calm voice from another world.

I gave her Rod's number. I spoke softly, ever so softly, fingering the growing lump on my chin.

The operator dialed and that robot purred in my ear Once, it rang. Twice. Be there! I prayed. Just this once, God, let him be there. He'll know what to do. Rod will know 8-9-10. My heart sank. Three more times and I hung up.

The police? What would I tell them? What story that would send them racing? Did it matter? As long as they came?

The house detective? Better still. It was his job and he was seconds away. I would tell him that I was being held in this room and I wanted to be escorted safely out of the building. I reached for the phone.

Splat! A hand whipped across the side of my face. I fell sideways on the bed. I sat up, rubbing my cheek. Remick stood leering down at me.

"Got any more tricks?" he said. "Try something else and see what happens, sister."

He got some gadget from his pocket and unscrewed the plate from the bottom of the phone. He disconnected the wires. He tucked the instrument under his arm. He went out, closing the door.

Well, he was alerted and that was bad. He wouldn't dare slap me unless I was under suspicion. The whole thing was falling apart.

I reached for my pocketbook. I hated to use the gun. Because once you have a gun in your hand all the cards are on the table. Until then you might keep them guessing. You might keep them in business long enough to catch them with their filthy hands in the pie.

Also, while a gun is a key that unlocks a lot of doors, you have to be ready to use *it.* A threat is not always enough. Especially if you're a woman. Chances are, with such a crew, before it's over you'll have to fire the gun. And afterwards you'll have to be able to justify such a shooting without friendly witnesses. If you can't, there goes your license.

And finally, if you're outnumbered and you ever have the gun taken away from you, you're dead.

So as I held the gun in my hand. I thought about it very seriously. In the end I put it away. Because another idea came to me.

I went out to the balcony and took a look at the stone partition, the wall which separated me from the second bedroom. The wall which Markos had scaled.

It was about ten feet high and most women would never make it. But I am agile and much stronger than I look. I am trained to meet physical situations head-on. It wouldn't be the first wall I had gone over.

I took off my shoes and squeezed them into my pocketbook. I did a practice jump, straight up, and missed. I tried again. Missed. The third time my hands caught the top of the wall. I just wanted to be sure I could do it.

Next I got some bobby pins from my bag and fixed my skirt and slip so that they were fastened up around my waist. A skirt, especially the sheath variety, can be a real problem when you need your legs free.

Now I held the bag between my teeth and I was ready. I had the distance measured and I made it on the first jump. I pulled myself up, up, until my chin was over. I got my leg up there and hooked my heel on the edge of the wall. In a moment I was sitting astride the top. I hauled the other leg over and eased down, jumped the remaining few feet.

I prayed that if that sliding glass door to the bedroom had a lock, it wasn't bolted. It wasn't. I slipped in. The room was dark.

I looked for a phone. In this room there wasn't one. Damn! Well, I hadn't counted on it. The door was open a crack. I listened and heard voices. I couldn't make them out. I figured that in time Remick would look in on me again. Maybe he had tipped Markos that my door was locked in the first place. Anyway, he would go in there and he would find me gone. For a minute he would search around and then he would report to the others. But first he might just catch on to the wall. And that would never do. I needed some kind of distraction that would keep him from thinking very much at all.

I went back to the balcony. I made another leap up the face of that wall, this time leaving my pocketbook below I caught the top and hoisted myself until my head was over. I faced towards the room and let out a giant scream. And then another. Sure enough, I heard Remick come bulling into the room. I dropped down and soon his feet scuffed on the other balcony. By this time I had my shoes on, my skirt was pulled down, the bag was in my hand. I leapt into the room and stood by the door.

Remick went thundering down the hall. I heard his shout.

"The goddamn bitch has jumped or something! I can't find 'er!"

Ahhhh. Just what I wanted. In a moment I saw them all go scampering past, into the other bedroom. That's when I raced out on my toes to the living room. I reached under the sofa and got the mini-tape. I dropped it into my bag. I ran for the door.

I had it open. I looked back once. They had caught on. Markos was in the lead, Tarino following. I slammed the door behind me, practically in their faces.

I went flying down that short flight of stairs, stumbling, recovering. I gained the corridor and pushed as fast as I could go for the elevators. The tight skirt hampered me. I looked over my shoulder. They were just leaping from the stairs. I knew they were going to catch me.

I rounded a bend and saw the elevator bank. No luck. The cars were all down on other floors and not a human being in sight. There were stairs but they would grab me before I made the first landing. I searched around frantically.

Suddenly a door opened—a room off a branch corridor. A thick-set balding man with glasses stepped out. I never lost stride. I had reached him before he pulled the door to. I crashed in He stepped back into the room with this astonished gaping expression.

"Well, f'Crissake, f'Crissake!" he said He sounded slightly loaded.

"Some awful man is after me," I said weakly. "He he tried to rape me. Will you please for God's sake, shut the door. And lock it, lock it!"

He gave me a kind of confused, hungry look and pushed the door. He bolted it

"Well, sure," he said. "F'Crissake. Poor kid. Stay here as long as you like. All night if you want. How 'bout a little drinky, huh?"

"No drinky," I said. "But thanks. Maybe later, huh? Right now my brother is waiting for me in the lobby."

"Your brother?"

I nodded. "He's a soldier. Home on leave. If he finds out some man was in my room—well, I just don't know what that big ape would do to me."

That sobered him a little. "What next then, honey?"

"Go out and see if there's anyone in the corridor. If not, ring for an elevator and come back."

He stalled, wiping his glasses with a handkerchief. "But I'll see you later, won't I, honey?"

"Of course, of course, dear man."

"Charlie. Charlie Gates."

"Charlie, then. Now hurry, hurry!"

He went out, first peeking up and down the corridor. He returned in half a minute.

"All set," he said. "The joint is deserted. I buzzed the elevator."

"Good, good! I can't thank you enough." I meant it. I went to the door.

"What's your name?"

"Angelica. Just call me Angel."

"You are, oh, you are!" He reached for one of my breasts. I reared back and he missed. I raised my hand to swat and changed my mind.

After all, he was a little lifesaver.

"'Bye, Charlie." I ducked out.

"Don't forget that drinky," he called after me. "Later, huh?"

I saw the elevator door open. "Don't wait up for me," I said, and hurried into the car.

I couldn't spot any of those hoods in the lobby. I moved on to the exit and out to the driveway. A cab was pushing up the little hill under the marquee. A young couple stood beside the doorman, watching it expectantly. I was about to head for the street when I saw Markos and Tarino. They were down on the sidewalk and they had also seen me. For a second they froze. Then they began to run.

The young woman was just bending herself to get into the cab. I shoved in front of her and fell on the seat. "Sorry," I said. "Emergency! The nearest hospital, driver!"

I slammed the door and the cab leapt ahead. I looked from the rear window. Markos, still in the lead, was reaching a long arm toward the trunk. He looked wild. His fingers grabbed air. He fell back, stopped altogether.

We turned sharply onto Collins Avenue, fled north.

I settled back in the seat and lighted a cigarette, puffing violently.

"Never mind the hospital, driver," I called. "Suddenly I feel better. I can't tell you how much better I feel."

I gave him my home address. The real one. I wouldn't go back to the Vanderwalt apartment. For a time Myra Vanderwalt would cease to exist. Because I had an idea her usefulness in this case was just about over.

I was never so glad to be just plain—Myra Bailey.

CHAPTER SEVENTEEN

ROD STRIKER

It was around twenty minutes after midnight when I got home. I was reaching for my keys when I heard the phone ringing. At least I thought I did. But after I got the door open and goddamn near broke a leg on that obstacle course to the bedroom, the line was deader than Alex Bell himself. The reason I was so anxious was that I figured it might be Myra. I hadn't heard a peep from her since the middle of the afternoon. Maybe that was because I was out most of the time.

Anyway, I gave her a call at that Vanderwalt hood-trap she has on the west side. We had a little code worked out so that if she had company I would know and we'd play wrong number. But she didn't answer and as usual I told myself to forget it, that she could damn well take care of herself. And as usual I didn't forget it, I worried. Nothing frantic. Just that chronic anxiety I carried around when we were out of touch for more than five or six hours. Things can happen—even to the Myra Baileys. One of these days, one of these nights… But if that time ever came, there were going to be some sad bastards on the other end of my fists. Myra and I are a lot closer than I'll ever admit—to her. And there are marriages which never get recorded in heaven or the Bureau of Statistics.

During the early part of the evening I had been to see Aunty Rumshaw. She had a two-bedroom house on the bay which cost seventy-five grand. Can you imagine paying seventy-five thousand for a one-story with two lousy bedrooms? Sure, I'll admit it was on that solid-gold-type waterfront property. And I'll admit you could drive a bus into the living room without breaking up the bridge game. But seventy-five G's! Cheez…

Over the garage there was a small apartment. A pair of servants lived up there, a man and his wife. They took care of everything but the grounds which were combed and clipped by an itinerant gardener. That means he also clipped a couple of dozen other houses in the neighborhood for around eighty a month apiece. He was a colored man and Mrs. R. told me that once he came by on a Sunday for his check and he was driving a new Cadillac that was so long it had two steering rigs, one to turn the back wheels. Man, I said, I'm gonna trade my gun for a rake.

But what we talked about mostly, of course, was Kim. Mrs. R. said that she and the boy friend, Howie, had decided not to wait to get married. Because of this trouble with Tarino. They had gone off secretly and hitched their little wagons to the same star, not even telling Aunty. Which made her pretty damn mad—until they promised to play the same trick on each other again in April. Only this time they would perform in church with all the dressing.

They had made some photostats of the license and the idea was to send a copy to Tarino. This would cause him to see the light and he would then cease forever his slimy underhanded tactics. End of trouble. Right away I understood what Massey had meant when he told me he had a perfectly legal maneuver up his sleeve to fix Eddie-boy.

It didn't make much sense. Why? Because hadn't there been a threat that if Kim got married, Aunty and/or the boy friend would fall dead one night? Yes, but this, said Massey, was a bluff. The minute Tarino saw the legal handwriting on the wall, he would give up, fold his tail and steal away.

Kim had agreed. At the time. But just as Howie was about to mail the document, she got cold feet. She was afraid. She wanted to wait a bit. She would handle Tarino in her own way, at her own time. Maybe his ardor would begin to cool if she appeared to go along with him awhile.

So now she was married and dating Tarino. Crazy. Just plain crazy! The goddamnedest case I ever had.

And naturally, Massey was steaming like a Turkish bath. He was wedded but not bedded. All the sorrows, none of the joys. His bride was out on lend-lease. God!

Well, to tell you the truth, I was just as glad that Kim had those cold feet. Better than cold dead bodies. And now I could finish Tarino off in my own style—b*efore* the fact.

After this revealing chitchat with Aunty Rum, I went out to see Ben Ulrich at his house. Ulrich was head of the Homicide Squad in the Second District. He used to be my boss—but I liked him any-way. We got along. So he built us a drink and then I pumped him for anything he knew about Tarino. Which wasn't too much and some of it second-hand. Because normally Tarino's type of operation fell under the jurisdiction of the vice detail. But I did get a few gems for consideration.

It was no secret that Tarino was running a B-girl racket. The only secret was why the department wasn't shutting him down. From time to time there had been one hell of a lot of complaints from suckers who had been taken. In these joints you'd get cheap booze watered-down at two bucks a copy—if you were lucky enough to be sober. Once a john got stiff, the price was all he could stand. With maybe a dozen drinks on the bill he couldn't remember ordering. While the cookie drank colored water or tea which went on the tab as solid hooch. Cute tricks like that and a few more, even including an oc-casional wallet snatch.

A lot of complaints and no action. Just promises. Sure, friend, we'll look into it, and back would come the report— Our man could find nothing wrong out there. And we have to catch them in the act, buddy.

Someone was getting paid off. Period.

There was also a rumor that Tarino was banking a big chunk of the bolita setup in town.

So what? I wanted more. A felony which could put Tarino in Rai-ford for a long stretch, not some rap that would cost him a fine and his license.

Nine times out of ten when a guy is running a couple of swindle houses like The Frolic and getting away with it, he's got some oth-er angles which sink a lot deeper. There's no such thing as a crook who's permanently happy with the take. If he clears a hundred grand a year, he wants to make it two. If he makes two, he wants four, and so on. Well, you can clean just so much from a given racket. So he branches out. And it's those branches you have to look for. Maybe his whole operation is just a cover. I thought this might be the case with Tarino. I had to find out.

Ulrich gave me some hints. There were no ex-cons on Tarino's payroll. But a few months ago his joints began to be hangouts for some very bad boys from other cities—especially the north. Now these hoods don't just drop in for coffee and doughnuts. For kicks they've got the loot to go to the best places. So they must be cooking up deals. They must be figuring a big haul in the back rooms.

Among these characters, said Ulrich, there was a wheel from Chicago, a fast-buck artist called Nick Markos. This guy had his fingers in a lot of dirty plums around the country. His front was a restaurant and bar supply house with outlets in half a dozen cities, including Miami.

Underworld pigeons sang a little song. The song told of the Markos warehouses being used as drops for stolen goods. Wholesale robbery with Markos as receiver and distributor to interested parties. That's the way the song went. But no one could prove anything.

When a Markos warehouse was to be raided he must have been tipped. For nothing was ever found. Lately, the warehouses of Nick Markos were becoming as impregnable as armored car barns. The new drops, such as the one in Miami, had only a single steel door, a huge affair, which was kept always locked. There were two windows, but these were high up, inaccessible and too small to admit a man. Thus, a surprise raid was out of the question. You'd need a tank to ram your way through the side of the building.

This was all that Ben Ulrich could tell me. Except that Tarino and Markos were thick, they had been seen together on more than one occasion. So it seemed obvious that Tarino had his hand in the Markos operation. Logically, he would be in charge of the Miami warehouse.

As I was leaving, I thanked Ben for the information. He was sorry he didn't have more. I told him it was plenty and I could use it. He said to be careful. I said I would, I certainly would.

He only laughed.

So I went on home and I thought I heard the phone ringing but when I picked it up the line was dead. And no Myra at the Vanderwalt trap. The whole business made me nervous. It was tough getting to sleep. But my God, you can't function without a little snooze now and then. So I finally conked off.

And then the doorbell rang. At two in the morning?

I answered with a gun in my hand.

But it was Myra.

"What the hell," I said, "are you doing here!"

And then I got a good look at her. She was a mess. There was a purple lump on her chin. She was pale. Her air must have been combed with a vacuum cleaner.

I pulled her inside and shut the door. I put my arms around her and kissed her.

"Oh, Rod," she moaned. "Oh, darling, what a night, what a night!"

"Sure, baby," I said. "I'll bet you had a beaut of a time. But you're safe now." I walked her to my sofa and we sat down. "Just tell me what that bastard did to you."

"Among other things," she sighed, "he scared me right back into Myra Bailey."

"Oh yeah? I'll fall on him. Like a brick wall. Tarino?"

"No," she said. "Not exactly."

"Who, then?"

"Markos. An ape by the name of Nick Markos."

CHAPTER EIGHTEEN

For a long time I just listened as Myra unfolded her sordid tale of the night. The more I listened, the madder I got. Only Myra's good sense kept me from blasting off for the beach to bust in that penthouse door and Markos' face. I wanted to ram that sadistic smile down his throat. But we were close to the answers, Myra reasoned. Too close to show our cards for the mere sake of revenge. And of course she was right.

"I don't think they'll quit now," I said. "I don't think they're running scared. Not yet. Markos had a small hunch about you. But that's not enough to stop whatever scheme he's got cooking. He'll figure you turned green after that balcony torture and you got out of there as fast as you could before he carried out his threats. Anyone who stole a hundred bucks from that creep and damn near died in the attempt would react the same way. Soon as he calms down, he'll see that. So I think we can still nail him and Tarino. It's a question of how."

"Don't forget the tape," she said.

"That's right, by God. Let's hear it!"

The box was so small there was no room for a playback stage inside it. But I had a tape machine in the apartment which was plugged into a big amplifier and three speakers.

I removed the tape and transferred it. I turned up the gain and we listened.

It was one hell of a disappointment. Those hoods must have moved to another part of the room and their voices were indistinct to read. But occasionally Markos shifted his position, as if he might be pacing, and at times we caught a few words.

Something about a yacht, Tarino's yacht, and how it was to be loaded with cases from a warehouse on the following night. Then there was a heated discussion of payment. Evidently Markos wanted a hundred grand now and the balance on delivery. Someone disagreed. Markos insisted. He won. And that was when he lowered his voice and we couldn't hear another word that we could understand.

"I'm sorry," said Myra.

"Don't be. How could you know exactly where those mugs were going to sit? From what you tell me, it's a big room. No, we got a lot here to think about."

"We might have had it all," said Myra, sipping the long shot of bourbon I had poured for her. She had fixed her hair and covered the bruise with powder. She looked more like her old self again.

"Tomorrow night I'll be down there, Myra. When they move those cases to the yacht, I'll be watching."

"Don't you know what time it is, Rod? It won't be tomorrow night. It'll be tonight. And I'll be right there with you."

"Oh no you won't. You've had it, kiddo."

"That's what you think, lover. Who's going to show you how to find that warehouse?"

"You'll draw me a map."

She shook her head. "Nope. I couldn't possibly. I don't remember the route. But I could find it. I think."

I gave her my know-it-all smile and went for the phone book. I hunted Markos Supply. Nothing doing. If they had a phone, it wasn't listed.

"Okay," I said. "You'll be along. But you'll wait in the car."

"Sure, Rod. With the motor running."

"The perfect gun moll," I said. "We'd have made headlines together."

"Well, darling, it's not too late, you know. Just say the word."

"Shut your swollen face and write down all the items you can remember on that inventory list."

I got paper and my ballpoint. For a minute or two she wrote. Then I studied the items.

"How about those bars?" she said. "I know he's supposed to be in the business of selling them. But twenty-six cases! Isn't that a lot of bars?"

"You bet your ever-lovin'. Especially at twenty bars per case. Ha! You'd have a case two stories high."

"Then what in God's name does it mean?"

"I have a hunch it means just what it says, Myra. Bars. But not the kind of bars you serve drinks across."

"Tell me."

"Can't for sure. I'm just guessing Listen, you'd better hit the sack, sweetheart. Tonight the wheel spins even faster and you'll need your wits."

"Why," she said at the door, "do we even bother with Markos when he doesn't figure in this case at all?"

"Because," I said, "Markos has a little lamb whose name is Tarino. And everywhere that Markos goes…"

"First time I ever heard Tarino called a lamb." She leaned over and kissed me.

"'Night," I said.

"Morning, Rod." She went off with a wave.

I climbed back into bed with the light on. For a few minutes I mulled over the inventory. Bars, bars and more bars. TMGs and GRs. What the hell… I folded the paper and set it on the night table. What the hell… I was reaching for the light when I got it! I snapped my fingers. It was so simple it had vanished with too much effort.

The light went out and I fell into a dark hole. I slept like a baby.

For three hours.

Then the phone rang. I was down on the canvas for the ten-count and they were trying to reach me with that stupid bell. What a joke. What a fog! I groped around and came up with the receiver.

"Yeah, yeah! What now."

"Rod! Rod Striker, is that you!"

"Mmmm?"

"Rod, for God's sake answer me, answer me!"

She was screaming into the phone. She was hysterical. It was Kim Rumshaw.

"This is Rod. Calm down, honey. Calm down and tell me what's up."

There was a pause and now when she spoke her voice came low and vibrato.

"Rod, I… I'm over at my Aunt's house. Will you please come to me? Oh hurry, hurry!"

"Sure. Sure, Kim. I'll be right there. Have you called the police?"

"No. But how did you—"

"It was obvious. And I'm sorry, Kim. Are you sure she's—"

"Yes, yes, she's dead. Shot."

And then she broke down. I told her to hold on, I'd be there in a few minutes. I hung up.

I looked at my watch. It was five minutes to six and still dark. I placed a call to Ben Ulrich.

Then I threw on my clothes and hurled myself out of the apartment.

I made it in six minutes.

The first police car had just arrived.

CHAPTER NINETEEN

Martha Rumshaw was in her bed. She might have been asleep. Until you saw the blood-soaked pillow and the hole in her head just above the left eye. She lay on her side, covered to the neck. She must have been asleep when it happened. Someone gave her a lead pill that would continue her sleep—forever.

A patrol car cruising in the area was first on the scene. Then came Lieutenant Ulrich and two of his boys from the homicide squad. These were followed by the medical examiner, the police photographers, the lab crew, and finally the reporters. Soon the place was swarming.

"Doc says she hasn't been dead much over two hours," Ulrich told me. "Three at the most."

He was standing at the foot of the bed making notes, a brown-haired, middle-sized guy of forty-three with small neat features and careful brown eyes. There was an air of dignity about him with a dash of humor in the set of his full mouth. He had a good bearing and though not a flashy dresser, he was fussy about his clothes, never used the climate as an excuse to slop around. Put a mustache on him and he would remind you of Tom Dewey a few years back.

He took me aside and he said, "Rod, I want you to tell me anything and everything you know about this case. You might have left out a few items last night, but now it's all important."

I gave him the complete scoop, including the latest from Myra. He made notes but, typical of him, he never raised an eyebrow. You could tell this guy that Markos was stocking his warehouse with stolen atom bombs and he'd probably say— A-bombs? Okay. How many and what size are they? Just give him the details.

"You think Tarino did this?" Ben asked me.

"No. Not personally. He just hired a gun to do it for him, that's all."

"Well," said Ben, "we'll find out one way or another. I'll have Tarino picked up in an hour. When he pulled this one he got deep into my territory. That was a mistake he's not gonna forget."

"What about Markos?"

"Unless he's part of this, I can't touch him. But I might just find somebody who can." He winked. "Any prints, Ben?"

"Nope. Just hers." He nodded towards the bed. "Not even a button on the floor. A neat job. Professional."

"How did he get in?"

"Easy. The Florida Room door. He poked a hole through the screen, reached a mitt inside and turned the knob. These houses are a joke. Any house is if a pro wants in."

"What about the servants over the garage?"

"Nothing, Rod. Didn't hear a sound. They were dead to the world."

"Okay," I said, "and thanks. I'm gonna have a talk with Kim Rumshaw. Hell, I guess it's Massey, now. Kim Massey."

"Later," said Ulrich. "She's in the study on the day bed. She's a mess. Perfectly calm one minute, goes to pieces the next. Better make it later."

Later was around one in the afternoon when Kim had gone back to her own apartment. Howard Massey, the bridegroom, was there. She was quite composed, he was nervous. With good reason, I found out.

They sat together, across from me on one of those facing sofas in her living room. Massey held her hand and looked remorseful. He felt that he was to blame for what had happened. Since they were married and he was a rather solemn type who would frown on any familiarity with his bride, I decided on the formal approach. No sense hinting that Kim and I had once been a little too cozy.

"Now, Mrs. Massey," I said, "I'd like to know just what happened last night. That is, if you still want me to continue on this case. It's only fair to tell you that since a murder has been committed, you'll have the full cooperation of the police. They'll investigate all the way."

"I know that," she said. "But my Aunt hired you and she would have wanted you to…to carry on to the end. She had great faith in you. And that goes for me, too. Howie?"

He looked at her, seemed to pull himself from a stupor. "Certainly," he said. "I'm all for it. I can't help feeling terribly guilty, Mr.

Striker. It was my idea to get rid of Tarino by sending him a copy of the marriage license." He held a hand over his face. I thought he was going to cry.

"Darling!" Kim said. "Please, please don't blame yourself. Whatever you had in mind, you did absolutely nothing about it. I was the one who showed Eddie Tarino the photostat. Please?"

"All right," he said in a broken kind of way. "All right, dear. It's too late now, anyway. Nothing will change it."

She turned to me. "Don't worry about your fee, Mr. Striker. My Aunt was very generous. I have some money of my own."

"Don't be silly," said Massey firmly. "Present your bill to me, Mr. Striker. My wife's debts are my debts."

I was a little embarrassed. I didn't give a damn where the money came from. "Now," I said. "You were with Tarino last night. At a party given by a Nick Markos. You had a fight with Tarino. Tell me about it."

"He had a few drinks," she said. "He was riding high on his ego. He began to get—affectionate. Oh, let's be honest. He wanted me to go to bed with him. Right there in that penthouse with all those people—"

"God!" said Massey. "Oh, God!"

"Well, that was the last straw. I had that photostat in my pocketbook and I had been feeling kind of belligerent, anyway. I was fed up. So on an impulse I'll regret for the rest of my life, I showed it to him."

"And what did he do?"

"He was astonished. He turned white. Then red with anger. He struck me across the face. It was the first time he ever touched—hit me. I fell down and he tore the paper up and threw the pieces at me. 'You think this will do you any good,' he shouted. 'You think so? Just wait and see.'

"Then he carried me into a bedroom and he tried to— But I kept fighting him off and he knew he would practically have to kill me. I think he was afraid to go too far." She looked at Massey. "I just don't want to talk about what he did. Nothing, really. But someone knocked on the door and that was the end of it. He rushed me outside of the apartment into the hall. He threw a ten-dollar bill at me. 'Get a cab and go home,' he said. 'I'll take care of you later, baby. See if I don't. I've got connections. I'll get that marriage annulled and you'll help me. You'll be glad to do it. You'll beg me for it. Now beat it!'"

"That was all he said?" I asked. "He didn't make any specific threats? About your Aunt? Or Mr. Massey?"

"Oh heavens, no. He never made any specific threats. He was too clever for that. He let someone else do his dirty work."

"So then you got a cab and you came home. Right?"

"Yes."

"What time was that?"

"I don't know exactly. It was close to one o'clock by the time I got here. Then I phoned Howie and he came right over. We talked for a while, trying to decide what to do next. He left and I went to bed. I couldn't sleep. I tossed for hours. Finally I got up and I called my Aunt. She didn't answer but I wasn't terribly worried because she was a heavy sleeper. She had one of those plug-in phones and sometimes she left it in the living room. I slept for an hour or two and then I called again. This time when she didn't answer, I went over."

"You told Lieutenant Ulrich it was a little after five-thirty this morning. Correct?"

"Yes."

"And did you notice anything unusual when you got there?"

"Nothing. I had my own key and I went right into the bedroom. It was dark and I looked and Aunt Martha seemed to be asleep. I called her name and when she didn't answer, I put on the light. And then I… I…"

She couldn't go on. She just doubled up, sobbing. Massey put his arm around her and made soothing noises. Abruptly she straightened and wiped her eyes. "Howie," she said. "Tell him what happened to you."

Massey got up and paced for a moment, wringing his hands. Though the day was warm, he had on a dark gray suit and he wore a tie. His eyes were gouged with circles of fatigue, his features seemed to sag. Gone was the Joe-college front, the bravado. He was just plain frightened. He looked years older. I liked him better without the cocky air.

"I live in an apartment near my office," he said. "It used to be my father's before he died. I was staying there with him. He and my mother were divorced years ago. My father left me the business, though at the time of his death, I was sales manager. The apartment is on the fourth floor and there's no way into it except by the door. I mean, the windows are not accessible.

"But after this nightmare began, I had a double lock installed. It just seemed like a good idea. Since these threats were made, I've never been more than half asleep. Sometimes lately I would jump out of bed in the middle of the night, wide awake, listening. And it would be nothing but the elevator door, or maybe someone passing in the hall, some noisy drunk coming home.

"But this morning about three-thirty something woke me and I lay there listening to an odd sort of scraping noise. I couldn't place it and so I got up and went to the door. Then I heard it very plainly. Someone was tampering with the lock. Trying to get in, of course.

"At first I was going to open the door and grab whoever it was. But I figured it was Tarino or one of his hoods and he would be armed. I didn't have a gun and to open that door without one could be suicide. So I called the police. While I was waiting for help, that noise went on and on until my nerves were raw. Finally I got a carving knife from the kitchen and stood holding it in the dark, ready for anything.

"A squad car arrived in about three or four minutes. But you could hear that goddamn siren a mile off. And at the first sound of it, the noise stopped. Something like twenty seconds later I heard a car start under my window. I looked out and a big convertible was roaring away from the curb."

"Cadillac?"

"Could have been, I don't know." He stopped pacing and sat down beside Kim. "What did the cops find?"

"Some tool had been used on the lock. It was plain enough. One of the officers took a statement and I told him the truth—that I had been threatened because of Kim. Threkel, I think his name was. Yes, Officer Threkel. He and his partner waited around while I called Bud Griffin, my service manager and a mighty tough character. Used to be a pro boxer. Bud said I could stay with him for the night and I drove right on over there." Massey looked sheepish. "Maybe it was sort of cowardly, but after that business with the lock, I couldn't make myself stay in that place."

"Not cowardly," I said. "Smart. Anything else?"

"No. Kim reached me at the office a little after eight. I went right out there. I hadn't phoned her about what happened because I didn't want to worry her. Stupid. I should have known that guy would head for her Aunt's next. But, oh God, it just never entered my mind that anyone would really kill her."

At which point Kim began to weep again and the atmosphere was so goddamn morbid I couldn't take it any more. So I left. But on the way out I told Massey he had better play it safe and go right on staying with his friend, Bud Griffin.

"Well, I don't know about that," he said. "It's time I moved in with my wife. Kim is through with Tarino. She'll never see him again. The only way she wants to see him is dead. So now anything can happen and she might need protection."

"She might," I said. "But I doubt it. You're the one I'm worried about. For reasons we both understand, your wife has been quite safe from the beginning, and I don't think she's in any danger now."

That's what I told him. Because an attack on Kim didn't make sense.

But in this business you learn not to believe in what makes sense. The hard way.

CHAPTER TWENTY

They couldn't hold Tarino. Not for long. Ulrich tried, but it didn't work. Tarino had been at The Frolic from about two A.M. until closing at four. He had been seated with Markos at one of his tables and he never left. The entire staff and even a couple of customers known to the girls, backed him. At five after four he was in an all-night beanery down the block. He fed his face and read a paper until nearly five. A short-order jockey and his helper would swear on a stack of wheatcakes.

Martha Rumshaw was murdered between two-thirty and four-thirty, according to the med examiner. His best guess was close to three A.M. Exit Tarino. A sharpie lawyer had him free in a couple of hours. He knew nothing, saw nothing, heard nothing. Naturally. He never threatened anyone in his whole life. Naturally. Kim was just "a friend." He had no special interest in her. Naturally.

Well, none of us were much surprised. Of course he would have a flawless alibi. And of course he sent his hired gun. Just a phone call would take care of it. The gun would catch hell for goofing up Massey's erasure. He'd be told to try again if he wanted his dough. Likely he'd lay off until the heat cooled and Massey got careless. One thing puzzled me. What made Tarino think that after he buried the Aunt and hubby, too, Kim would fly into his arms? Unless he was a hopeless egomaniac or a total idiot, he would have some reason to expect a little cooperation. It would be mighty damn interesting to know that reason. I was going to give it a lot of thought.

Meanwhile, there was work to be done. Put Tarino in an eight-by-ten cubicle with floor-to-ceiling bars and find out which of his playmates pulled trigger for him, that's all. Nothing to it.

Myra found the Markos warehouse in daylight. We spent part of the late afternoon hunting it down. She had never been too familiar with that district and it was a job. We didn't stop. We slid right on past the place and came back after dark.

I needed a look-out while I cased the building. So Myra sat in my car half a block away around the corner of a side street. She had my binoculars and could spot anyone approaching, even without them. She was to beat the horn—one short and one long if there was trouble.

I crept up on the warehouse. It was dark. I knew it was early for Tarino and Markos to be hauling their freight to the yacht. But there might be a guard and I was quiet as a barefooted Indian.

I saw the two little windows up there; way up near the eaves and much too small. I could bet they were spy-proof, just admitting light. And if that wasn't enough, they were barred.

I paused at the big steel door. I combed the goddamn thing top to bottom and couldn't find so much as a handle, let alone a lock. There had to be another way in so I toed around the building, searching as I went. Nothing. A roach couldn't get in that place without the password. Not even the Florida variety—and they've got wings.

Then I remembered that Myra had said there must be a bell to signal inside and I went back to the door. Since the fortress appeared to be unguarded, I took a chance and used my pencil flash. Damned if I could find anything remotely like a button.

I had to give up and go back to the car.

"What luck?" said Myra.

"The kind that goes with a two-leaf clover. It's Fort Knox without guards. But who needs guards?"

"Great. So how do you get in, Rod?"

"Got a few sticks of dynamite you can spare?"

"Sorry, I left them in my other purse."

"That's no excuse. A lady always comes prepared."

"Yes, sir. And what do we do now—sir?"

"We wait. Know any games?"

"How about rugby?"

"Make it soccer. Spelled s-o-c-k h-e-r!"

"Okay. But I play rough," she said. "Remember?"

"Mmmm. Skin diving?"

"That's no game."

"It is the way I play it."

"Oh, shut up."

I did. We waited. It was a long wait.

Ten thirty-five. A Chevy sedan rolled past and braked before the warehouse. I couldn't see anyone in the Chevy but the driver. I used the glasses to make sure. The guy cut his lights and sat. I figured this one was a little early for the rendezvous. Or the others were late. In any case, he got bored and left the car in less than ten minutes. He went towards the warehouse.

I wasn't far behind him.

He didn't stop at the door. He went around the building and disappeared. I was going to follow him when I heard a beautiful sound. That big steel door was rolling upwards. He had touched the magic gismo in some secret place. Contact!

I heard him coming. But he wasn't fast enough, because I had ducked in that door and crouched behind a crate before he rounded the corner. In a moment there was the not-so-beautiful sound of the door closing again, locking in place.

Then lights flashed dimly overhead and there was the hollow clip of his feet going away on cement.

I peeked around the crate and watched. There was a small office in one corner and he was headed towards it. He went in and closed the door. Light winked behind glass.

I crawled around among those crates and had a look. Wood sections had been removed for inspection and it was a cinch to see inside. Easy, too easy. Especially since the crates contained exactly what the man was supposed to be selling—big kitchen ranges, coffee urns, mammoth refrigerators and other such giant knickknacks for the trade.

Not at all what I had in mind.

I moved behind those crates towards the office. Loosely speaking, the equipment formed a ring around the big room. The huge center of the floor was vacant. Why? The only logical answer was that the space was needed to store other merchandise. What kind? And where the hell was it?

I got close enough to that office so that I could see practically all of it through the glass in the door. There was a desk, the usual filing cabinets, a couple of chairs. Otherwise, the room was empty. I mean, that guy just wasn't there!

I bent low and got closer. I looked again. By God, it *was* empty.

Now that was impossible. Because I had seen him go in and I had been gluing my eyes to that room all the time, all the way, as a precaution. And I could swear he never came out.

I waited about a minute and then I pulled my .38 from the holster and quietly opened the door. Yup, empty. The door had a bolt inside and I shoved it in place without a sound. Nothing like giving yourself a little extra time in case of emergency.

I set the gun on the desk and was reaching for a drawer when I saw the phone. The unlisted job. For a moment I thought of calling Ulrich and telling him I was locked in this goddamn tomb with no way out that I understood. The fact is, I would have called him for sure if I had found item one that was incriminating. But you can't arrest a man because he's got an electric, self-locking door on his barn. And besides, the type of goods I was hunting would not fall under Ben's domain. I had other, more casual friends in the department but they wouldn't go out on a limb for me. After all, I had no official status and I was trespassing, plain and simple. The hell with it.

I had my mitt on the middle drawer when I heard a sound. A distant hum, an electric motor opening a door. I grabbed the .38 from the desk and went to peer into the outer room. Couldn't see a damn thing. Steel door still closed, no one about. Anyway, the sound had stopped. Which was no relief at all. It was weird.

Oh, Christ, I thought. This time I've done it I've fallen in over my head.

That was true. Because at the very second I was about to turn around, hard metal poked the back of my neck and someone said, "Drop it, bastard. Fast!"

I mean it, this guy was actually behind me in a locked empty room… He couldn't be? Don't argue with success, brother. He was there!

I dropped the gun. The damn thing was cocked and it went off. Wham! The slug zinged around the room like an angry lead bee. It had the sound of opportunity. But this was a very cool character. He just jammed that barrel another inch into my neck, pushing my nose against the glass of the door.

"Dumb son-of-a-bitch," he cursed.

"You said drop it, buddy."

"Hands behind your head!"

I obeyed. He pawed over me, backed off, said, "Turn around."

I did. He was a burly guy with a parrot beak and a pocked face.

He wore tan GI slacks and a dark short-sleeved sport shirt. He had muscles like hawsers—to moor the Queen Mary. There was a tattoo on one forearm. Nothing original. A belly dancer.

He was a perfect mate to the guy described by Massey as the one who gave him a thumping over. His muscles didn't scare me at all. But something else did. He was leveling Mr. Thompson's idea of a very portable machine gun. The kind that spits .45 slugs a lot faster than you can dodge them. This sort of weapon can give you a gutted feeling like few others.

"Who are you, bastard? And what's your game?"

I didn't answer.

"Your wallet. Toss it on the desk. That goes for the rest of your junk, too. Turn them goddamn pockets inside out."

I emptied my pockets but he didn't seem interested in anything but the wallet. He gave it a going over in such a way that he never really took his dirty eyes off me.

"Private snooper, eh?" He sat on the edge of the desk, sneering. "You're dead, you know that? You're already dead, buster."

I knew he was right. The stuff these boys were pushing spelled death in any language. To stand where I was meant you knew too much.

"You make a mistake with me and you'll be the dead one," I bluffed. "How the hell do you think I got in here? I'm doing a job for Eddie Tarino."

"Oh yeah? Is that right, now?"

"That's right."

He looked unconvinced but a flicker of doubt touched his ugly pan.

"What kind of job for Eddie Tarino?"

"Sorry, friend. I'm a clam. Those are my orders."

"Yeah? A clam, huh? Listen, wise guy. Eddie don't hire punks like you. Don't con me, bastard."

"Sometimes," I said, "Tarino will hire punks like me to watch punks like you."

At that moment his eyes flicked left and down. I followed the direction and right away a lot of things became clear. My Christ, there was a goddamn hole in the floor in a corner of the room. A square section of the cement flooring yawned and a ladder descended. The hole would just admit a man, the area so small I had missed it just now in the excitement. Of course the hole wasn't there when I entered the office. Because the guy had triggered a motor which closed the section after he went below.

"You know what's down there?" he said.

"Sure. Toys for Carga's children."

"You're very goddamn funny."

"I told you I was in. But don't take my word, fella. Ask Tarino."

He glanced at the phone and I coiled myself for the big gamble. There are times when you have to shoot dice with death or crap out by default This was one of them.

"Go ahead," I taunted. "Go ahead, call Tarino."

While he hesitated a moment longer, I wondered if by some idiot luck, Myra had heard that shot. What a joke. Those walls would hold the sound of a bomb.

"Hurry it up," I snapped. "We're on the same payroll and I've got work to do. C'mon, c'mon! Call Tarino."

That did it. He shrugged. His expression was damn near apologetic. He reached for the phone. And in the instant that he lowered the barrel of that Thompson just enough, I sprang forward and climbed all over him.

The gun came up and fired one quick burst that blew the glass out of the door and hurled crazy tinkling splinters into the warehouse. But I had snaked around the barrel and I was in close, hammering on that bent nose, straightening it out with the first fracturing blow.

The gun clattered to the floor and his head snapped back and I thought he was finished. But this guy loved a fight and pain was just a short fuse to explode him into action. He rolled and leaped off the desk to his feet. He came crouching towards me with his bloody mash of a nose drooling down his shirt. His eyes were slits and his fists were great knotty clubs anchored to bulging pistons of muscle. Now he saw the gun on the floor and made a quick move to reach for it.

That was only a dodge to get me in close. But by the time I found out, I had hurled myself at him and he had danced away to clobber the side of my head with a frozen ham that numbed my whole skull and damn near blew the lights out No more of that, I decided. And when he followed it up with a rush, I gave him a judo chop in the apple with one hand and a beauty in the gut with the other. When he doubled, I chopped the back of his neck and kneed him in the face for good measure. He began to fold and I kicked in a rib or two so he wouldn't change his mind. He didn't.

He cooled the hard way, the dirty way. But clean living will get you nothing but lilies from a hood. And the best hood next to a dead one is one that's half-dead.

Well, this guy was down on the cement canvas and he wasn't going to rise in any hurry. I always carry bracelets when there might be trouble, and just to make sure he was cozy, I cuffed his hands behind his back and under a leg of the desk.

I picked up my .38 and gave it to my holster. Then I took the Tommy and went down those stairs. I saw plenty of light below before I got to the bottom.

This cave down there was as big as the one above, though not as high to the ceiling. It was spread with rows and rows of cases—the type I knew I was hunting. But what really had me gaping was the sight of two ten-ton trucks in the center of the floor. I couldn't understand how the goddamn things got down there. Not until I saw the ramp leading right up to—the ceiling? What else? The ceiling was also the floor above and it must slide back to let those trucks out. How, was a problem I didn't have time to investigate.

I discovered a whole mess of tools on a bench in a corner and in a couple of minutes I had pried half a dozen of those cases open.

I found what I expected.

BAR's. Browning Automatic Rifles.

TMG's. Thompson Machine Guns.

GR's. Garand Rifles, Model M-1.

Now you can't buy that stuff and you don't find it lying around. So I knew the weapons had been stolen from government armories and maybe a couple of army posts, too. It was a giant haul and they must have been gathering it a long time from a good many parts of the country. I didn't know where it was headed but I had a pretty fair idea. This all added up to a very big rap for Messrs. Tarino and Markos—and friends.

There were cases of .45's and other assorted hand guns, much easier to come by. There were some light machine guns, caliber .30. And also a few heavies, .50 caliber. Ammunition to spare for everybody. For all I knew there were grenades and flame throwers. There wasn't time to ask all those boxes.

Well, I started upstairs to get to that phone. But half way, I caught on that I had delayed just a little too long. Because when I raised my head to look for that opening, it was gone. The floor had closed. I had a hunch it didn't close by itself. And my friend with the broken beak was helpless. So guess who?

I almost smiled when I thought about having enough guns and ammunition to fight a minor war. But the smile didn't quite come off.

Because just then the lights vanished and I was alone, sealed tight in the dark.

CHAPTER TWENTY-ONE

It was a hell of a fix to be in. Just before I went down the stairs I had grabbed my wallet from the desk. But I was in a hurry and figured to go right back up, so I left the rest of the stuff the hood made me toss from my pockets. That included my pencil flash, and my lighter. I don't carry matches. So I was *really* in the dark.

I was surrounded by a sea of ammunition. But I didn't have a prayer of finding the right shells for my two guns. If I ran out, that was it.

If there was a light switch anywhere close, I hadn't found it. Ditto, the switch to open that concrete panel. These boys had a bad habit of hiding the ways in and out of a place. Maybe they weren't trying too hard down here. But in the dark you could grope for an hour. Something told me I wasn't going to have near that much time. And it was even possible that they had yanked a fuse that would cut this branch of current.

There was just one thing in my favor. Only a man at a time could descend those stairs. I could pick him off with the Thompson. That meant nobody could come down, but then I couldn't go up either.

So I was still worried. Plenty.

Then I got an idea which was so simple I wondered why they hadn't thought of it, too. The trucks! Those babies had headlights…

I moved forward carefully. My eyes were growing accustomed to the darkness and I could see the vague outline of piled cases. I stepped around them and after a time I came to an open space. The trucks should be just ahead. They were.

I climbed into the cab of the nearest one. I saw that there was a small problem. The trucks faced the ramp and I needed light in the other direction. Well… I fished around for a key in the ignition slot. It was there. So I could back the truck into position. No, I couldn't. The sound might reach above and I didn't want to give anything away. The best thing was to cut the lights in and catch a certain amount of illumination by deflection. It would be enough.

Again I groped over the panel, found the light switch. I was about to give it a pull when I heard a sound. It didn't take me long to identify that sound. I had heard a couple like it in the past hour. Somewhere a motor was spinning. This one had more guts. It set up a whine you couldn't miss.

I dropped my hand from the dash and got the chopper in place so that the barrel poked out a window. Hell, I didn't know which way to aim it or what was going to happen next. But I like the feel of the damn thing at the ready.

It seemed to me that very slowly the complexion of the darkness changed. It got lighter. Not much, but a little. And that was a clue.

I leaned out the window and looked up. Sure enough, they were opening the really big panel, the concrete section overhead which cleared the ramp for truck passage above. I keep saying "they" because I knew damn well that by now the others had arrived, in force, for the loading.

Anyway, I got the picture, the plan. They must have awakened pock-face and he told them what happened and who I was. They knew I was armed and they couldn't climb down those narrow stairs. But the ramp was wide and they could scramble down it in numbers to knock me off in short order. They were counting on surprise. They didn't know I had figured the setup.

It took awhile for that big section to slide back. Maybe half a minute or more. The whole time I had my eyes fastened to the top. I would see them first. In fact, they wouldn't see me at all in the cab.

Soon enough, three or four shadows appeared above. They started down the ramp. One at a time, not bunching together and crouched low. I leaned out and drew a bead on the first guy, eased my finger against the trigger.

Then I changed my mind. It was no good unless I caught them all together down at the bottom of the ramp. At the first shot the others would scatter back above and I'd be in about the same spot. They'd seal me in my prison again, or they'd wait for me to go up and then pick me off from hiding. No good. And what if three or four guys came down and the rest waited above? I didn't know how many there were. God almighty!

Think! Think!

Well, three guys made it to the bottom and crouched in a huddle, whispering. I could make them out as my eyes were now sharp in the dark and there was a pale flush of light from above. I had those three lined up approximately on the other end of that barrel. You don't need a lot of accuracy with a machine gun. You can spray an area and take everything in it with a little luck.

But hoods or not, did I want to butcher three of those bastards in cold blood? And if so, would it be over? There just had to be more than three for this kind of operation. I was sure of it. And even a half-baked lieutenant doesn't put all his troops under fire at once. He keeps some in reserve. Yes, there must be others above.

Think! Think! One mistake would be one too many.

I let those three pass. They separated and moved among the cases. Then I made up my mind. A long shot and damn risky. But it had a chance.

I fumbled around in the dark, touching gadgets, making myself familiar with them. I knew about trucks. I had driven several in the army, a couple of civilian jobs, too. So I got ready and then I hit the starter and prayed. Don't miss, you big bastard, don't miss!

She caught on the first couple of turns and growled for action. Thank God for warm climates and ditto motors. I shoved in gear and fed gas, careful not to stall. We roared to the bottom of the ramp and ground upwards.

I heard the first shots. They came from behind. Too late and harmless against the big rump of the truck. I couldn't hold the machine gun, needed both hands for the wheel.

The ramp had an easy curve, a half spiral. I reached the turn, picking up speed. This baby had plenty under the hood, power to spare for climbing. Now I gave the light switch a yank to blind any goons at the top. The headlights flared around the swing and up. They caught three gorillas in various stages of frenzied movement, mostly taking aim, one with a sawed-off shot gun. I ducked so low as I passed, the truck was on automatic pilot.

Wham! The shotgun blast blew the windshield in on top of me. Glass showered the back of my neck. Bullets spattered the cab, too high. And then the hoods were behind. I jerked up.

That huge steel door, closed of course, loomed thirty feet ahead of me across the floor. I had lost speed going over the top of the ramp and I didn't know, I wasn't at all sure…

I stepped hard on the gas. But a truck doesn't exactly leap ahead like a car.

"Myra!" I shouted. "Here I come!" Crash!

A sound of metal crumpling against metal. The tinkle of glass. A dull, thundering echo. A complete, violent stop.

I was slammed forward. I flipped over the wheel. It crushed against my chest, threatened to break, didn't. My head beat against the top rim of the windshield and for a moment I was numb, brainless. Oblivion was a friend beckoning. I fought it with a lifetime of accumulated discipline. To pass out was as good as a bullet in the brain. I shook my head. It cleared.

I was in total darkness. The crash had pulverized the headlights. But I could see the big door. It bulged outward, but it had held. Not enough speed—and one hell of a door!

Dead issue. I didn't waste a second. I found the Thompson on the floor, scooped it and climbed out of that truck on the run. My shoulder met the hard bone of another shoulder. We both spun. I recovered and scurried on. I had lost direction, didn't know where I was going in that blackout. I hid behind a crate to get my bearings. I heard shouts, feet pounding up the ramp. Christ! I was still trapped in that tomb. With six gun-happy, kill-crazy bastards!

But my sense of direction returned, my brain cleared, and I had one last idea. It depended on this darkness remaining. Just a minute more. One more minute of confusion....

I whispered forward on the ramp side of the warehouse, crate to crate. I heard voices at the track. Loud and clear.

"Where'd the son-of-a-bitch go?"

"Can't find him, Nick." (Nick Markos?)

"All right, all right. Hit the goddamn lights, Remick! The rest of you take cover. C'mon! Take cover!"

Feet scuffling. A flash winking on and off.

I let the sounds hide my movements. I ran. Jesus, did I run! I got to the last crate before the office. Twenty feet. And then the lights went on.

Silence. What silence! You could hear a pin drop.

Well, there just wasn't a choice. I crouched down and launched myself towards that office, zigzagging all the way. Five bullets and a shotgun blast ripped after me. Lead chipped stone, climbed, drilled the office door in front of me. I bellied down and sent one quick burst in the right direction. I saw a couple of heads duck back. I jumped for the door, ploughed inside, slammed and locked it, got out of range.

There were more shots and I answered with the chopper, firing through the upper part of the door where the glass was gone. I knew I didn't have many more rounds and this was it. A machine gun will keep a whole platoon down, but a lot of nuts will run at you in the face of a .38. There was open space between those punks; and the office and I could have held them an hour with ammunition. But what I needed now was a good minute, not much more.

I went over to the desk. Yup, the phone was still there. There are times when a phone can look better than a chorus line of lush nudes. This was the time. I started to pick up the receiver. And then I looked down at the cord.

It wasn't connected? Yes it was, by God. Sweetly as ever. No one guessed I would ever see that office again.

I listened for the tone, dialed frantically. This was one number I knew well. A voice like a yawn answered. I didn't get the name. Because I couldn't hear above a new volley of shots. But I knew it wasn't Ulrich.

I shouted his name and begged for speed. He came on. I damn near wept.

"Rod Striker," I yelled. "Don't say a goddamn word, Ben. Just listen!"

I held the receiver towards the door. Two beats and the shots came again.

"Hear that? There's a war at Markos' warehouse. Six hoods and one poor slob of a civilian—me! You got thirty seconds to bail me out Understand!"

"Read you, Rod. Give location." Talk about calm! This guy sounded like he was asking where to find the bingo game. I told him.

"Coming with the whole squad," he said. "Hold on, boy."

"It's a tomb with a steel door and I'm locked in, Ben. Bring something to blast that door. No kidding! And hurry!"

I hung up.

Then I picked up the gun and hugging the wall, took a quick squint. I saw movement. They had reached the last crate before the office. I let them have a long burst, and the gun was empty. I tossed it on the desk and plucked the .38 from the holster. I was thinking about Myra. What in God's name did she figure was going on? I found out soon enough.

There was a pause in the shooting and then someone was shouting. I heard my name echoing out there.

"Striker! Hey, Striker! Hold ya fire and listen, bastard. We got ya girl. That Myra bitch. You give up or we'll plug 'er brains out and feed 'em to ya!"

Then I heard Myra screaming, "Rod, Rod! Don't do it. They'll kill me anyway!"

She said something else, but it died as if a hand was clamped over her mouth.

"You got twenty seconds, Striker! Throw them guns out first!"

So close to the end and now this. Well, close gets no prize. You might as well miss a million miles. Hell, I had no choice. I tossed the guns and went out behind them with my hands raised.

Pock-face greeted me first. He was behind the shotgun. He was a dried-blood mess. Swollen and battered. The cuffs were still on his wrists, but they had been hacked apart. He wasn't smiling much.

A hulking youngish-looking character with reptilian eyes was next. He had Myra squeezed up under the arm, practically lifting her off her feet. Her face was crumpled with the pain of it. Then four others came out, among them a greasy Latin and a guy they called Nick, who was giving the orders. I knew it was Markos.

Tarino? He just wasn't there.

"You had a good time for yourself, eh, smart boy?" said Markos. "Well, the play is over and I got all the chips, huh?" He gave me a back-handed whack across the face, and I took it. For Myra's sake. And also because both barrels of that shotgun were practically jammed up my nose.

"Let the girl go," I said. "You can have your kicks with me."

"We'll have our kicks with you anyway, friend. Got any other offers?"

Pock-face held out his hand. "The key, bastard," he said.

I gave it to him and he unlocked the cuffs and tossed them aside. Then he said, "What'll we do with them, Nick?"

"What you think?" said Markos. The other four stood licking their chops with anticipation.

"Just let me have this one," said Pock-face, jamming the gun in my belly.

"You and Remick," said Markos. "Take them down below. Give it to them right in the face—both barrels."

"What about the goddamn noise?" asked the one holding Myra. Apparently he was Remick.

"Down below, who hears, stupid?" said Markos.

"No, I mean the racket up here just now. Crissake, it sounded like Carga and Castro having at it in a revolution."

"You shut up!" threatened the greaseball. Of course he was Carga.

"Yeah," said Markos. "That's right. Maybe a couple of hundred shots. The sound could of leaked. We better shove off. Okay. Roll up that door and we'll take these two along to the yacht. They'll keep an hour."

"How about the loading, my guns?" said Carga.

"Not tonight," said Markos. "Have a look at that truck. All right, move, Remick! Get that door up."

"I'll try," said Remick. "Truck's mashed against it."

"Don't give me talk," said Markos. "Do it!"

Remick shrugged, let go of Myra and went off. Myra rubbed her arm and tried to smile at me.

In a moment the door groaned upward. About four feet. And stopped.

Remick came back on the double.

"Can't raise it another inch, Nick," he said. "Won't go up and won't come down, either. Goddamn thing is jammed."

Markos went livid. His mouth fell open, he tried to say something and the words never came. His head was cocked, he was listening. I heard it, too. The lovely music of sirens in chorus. The lead voice was just blocks away.

I turned to Myra. "You hear something?" I said.

She didn't answer.

But you could hang your wash on her smile.

CHAPTER TWENTY-TWO

The rats ran out of their hole and right into the arms of the cops. There was some shooting. Remick took a slug in the shoulder. Then Markos got one in the thigh. It sent him down and he didn't get up. I suppose that took the heart out of the others because they quit in a hurry. One cop was hit. A bullet grazed his side, nothing serious.

Funny thing. Those guys had enough weapons and ammo to hold off the entire police force. Instead they ran. Maybe it was that jammed door which discouraged them. And maybe they had no more guts than most hoods when the chips are on the line. I'll take that last for an explanation.

The truth came out soon enough down at headquarters. Especially after the FBI found they had jurisdiction and they took over most of the investigation.

As I had figured, the greater part of those guns were stolen from government armories. Some were hijacked from trucks making deliveries. Others disappeared from an army post—with inside help. Quantities of hand guns were swiped from stores and hock shops.

For the hoods it was Operation Money. For Carga it was Operation Castro. He wasn't starting a revolution to bring down the bearded dictator as I had thought. On the contrary, he was a self-appointed Castro agent. Castro had won by force and he had to hold by force. He had trouble within his regime and counter-revolutions threatened his island from a dozen launching points which surrounded him in the Caribbean. His little empire was shaky and the Commie-haters were ready to pull it down. He was even prepared to arm hordes of sympathetic civilians.

So he needed guns. All types, especially small arms. And these were becoming harder and harder to find. Enter Carga.

Carga was a sugar baron, enormously wealthy. He spent much of his time in the U. S. He had contacts. He could get guns, stolen guns. And what's more, he had the dough to pay about three times what they were worth if they could be bought on the market. Enter

Markos.

It was possible that Carga had made a deal with Castro to keep his holdings in exchange for guns. We might never find out. Because Carga claimed that while he was admittedly rounding up arms for his country, he had not the least sanction from his government. In fact, said Carga, Castro had no knowledge of the plan and Carga was an independent patriot aiding his people in the only way he knew how.

It could have been true. And if not, who's to deny it?

Other stores of arms had gone to Cuba via Tarino's charter yacht. The charter business was the cover. This was to be the last shipment. And speaking of Tarino, he was caught on board the yacht with two of Carga's "associates." It looked like the end of the line.

But it wasn't

No gun was found on Tarino. And none of the weapons taken from the hoods fired slugs that matched the bullet which killed Martha Rumshaw. This bullet was believed to be from a .32 automatic. So the case wasn't solved. And maybe a hired killer who had nothing to do with the arms-running was loose—and ready to kill again.

To top it off, on the following afternoon, Tarino was released on bail. If he had been in on that shoot-up at the warehouse he would have been held like the others. But he wasn't caught with the goods, the evidence was circumstantial and he denied everything. Of course. His offense was bailable and raising the dough was no problem for him. In short, that boy was out. And while he was out he could operate. Period.

It wasn't an hour after Eddie-boy got his freedom that Kim Massey was on the other end of my phone.

"He's at it again, Rod," she said. She called me Rod Whenever Massey was out of hearing.

"He—who?" I said. "And at what?"

"Tarino, of course. He just called me."

"What's his pitch?"

"Well, I didn't hear all of it because I hung up on him. He wanted to see me. I told him I'd be glad to go down and see him—in the morgue. I accused him of murdering my Aunt. He said that was silly. He was no killer. He wouldn't do a thing like that. I should stop listening to fairy tales from punks who were trying to frame him.

"I said if he ever called me again I'd have him arrested. He laughed at me. He said, 'We'll be traveling the same hot road together in a couple of days, baby. You'll wise up. Wait and see.'

"That was when I hung up. But I'm scared, Rod. I really am."

"Keep cool, gal," I said. "You just relax. I'll find that guy and this time I'll see that he leaves you alone for good. He's in plenty of trouble and if he takes one more step in your direction, I might be able to have him thrown back in the pokey—no bail. At least I can make him believe it Don't worry, you'll be off the hook."

"Oh thanks, Rod, thank you so much. I can't tell you how grateful I'd be."

"Forget it, Kim. I'm just doing a job and I'm being well paid. Although last night I wondered if there was enough money in the whole goddamn world. Anyway, sit tight and calm. You'll hear from me."

I went over to Tarino's house. He wasn't there. I tried his clubs and a few other dives he hangs out in. I asked questions everywhere. No Tarino. I went home and I called Kim to tell her not to open her door to anyone, unless she was sure who it was.

"Listen," she said breathlessly. "I've been trying to get you for an hour. I can't find Howie."

"When did you see him last?"

"At noon for lunch. He's been staying with me, you know. I wanted him to move his clothes and everything. He went home to pack. He was to be here for dinner two hours ago. I called his apartment. No answer. I tried the auto company. No answer. I tried Marilyn Jackes, his girl-Friday at the office. She had no idea where he was. Honestly, I've been frantic. Just frantic!"

"It doesn't look too good, at that. Do you have a key to his apartment?"

"Oh, God, oh, God! You don't think—"

"I don't think anything, Kim. Just taking the first steps. What about the key?"

"No, I don't have one. But I think there's one with a bunch of other keys on a ring in his desk at Massey Auto Sales."

"Is anyone there at this hour?" It was close to eight.

"No, they're closed. But Miss Jackes has a key to get in and she's home."

"Good. Where does she live?"

"One block east of the showroom on the same side of the street.

Second floor, apartment 2G."

"Okay. I'll hop over there and call you back. Now listen—don't open your door to anyone unless it's your husband or me. Not anyone! Understand?"

"Yes. I… I understand. But I'm frightened."

"Just keep that door locked with the chain latched and you'll be all right. See you."

I hung up.

CHAPTER TWENTY-THREE

Marilyn Jackes had her apartment in an ancient building of yellow brick. I took the stairs and rang the bell of 2G. She was a long time answering. But when she finally came, it was rewarding. She was wearing a transparent peignoir and very little else. Marilyn Jackes was that demure-looking redhead in Massey's office—the one with the classy assy.

"Oh," she said, kind of startled. "You're the man who—"

"That's right, Miss Jackes. I'm the man who. We met at Mr. Massey's office. Remember? Rod Striker."

"Yes," she said. "Of course. The detective!"

"Could I come in a moment?"

"Well…is there any particular reason why, Mr. Striker?"

"Yeah. Just now I looked at you and I said to myself— Gee whiz, I'd sure like to go into that girl's apartment."

"I'm afraid I don't understand."

"I'm looking for your boss. Have you seen him?"

"Mr. Massey?"

"If he's your boss. Even if he isn't."

"Well, no. I haven't seen him since early this afternoon."

"You have no idea where he is?"

"He said he was going to do some packing and wouldn't be back to the office. That's all I know."

She shifted positions and the gown fell away from her leg. It was quite a leg.

"Mrs. Massey is worried," I said. "He was due at her place a couple of hours ago. She wants you to get the key to her husband's apartment from the office so that I can go have a peek in there."

"How would that help, Mr. Striker?"

"Look, you're a nice girl and you've got lots to recommend you." I took another glance at those recommendations. Yup. She had them. "But please don't ask questions. This could be an emergency. Just get that key for me."

"All right," she said dubiously. She stepped back to let me pass.

The furniture was rather beat up and dying of age. But she had dressed the place with color and frills. The only thing in that living room worth over fifty bucks was probably the stereophonic player in a corner. Music pulsed from it with a sweet clarity.

"I'll have to dress," she said. "It'll take a minute or two."

"Couldn't we have a little dance first?" I couldn't resist teasing her. She was the sort who pretends modesty and virtue with a body that makes a liar out of the face.

She just stood there with her mouth open so I grabbed her and waltzed her around the room. We weren't doing the same steps, but it was a crazy little kick while it lasted.

"Please!" she said.

I paused, holding her tight. Togetherness.

"Mr. Striker, I thought this was an emergency."

"There are two emergencies. This is the other one."

She gave me a tense, flickering smile. I let her go.

"What are you doing between cases?" I asked her.

"Pardon?"

"Oh hell, get dressed, Miss Jackes. One emergency at a time and first things first."

She left the room in a swirl of movement, her fanny waving another of those haughty good-byes. The fun was over. There never seemed to be time for it.

I walked restlessly about the room. I looked out the window. A back apartment overlooking a fire escape, an alley, garbage cans. Lights from other windows cast patches of yellow over the dreary scene, draping it with illumination and shadow. For a full minute I sat on the sill of the open window and thought about Tarino and Martha Rumshaw...

Suddenly, I lost my sense of humor.

I left the window, moving about with a coiled feeling of urgency. I paused in the kitchen doorway, saw the tap, helped myself to a glass of water. Dishes were scattered about, unwashed.

"Sorry, it's such a mess, Mr. Striker."

I looked up and she was standing in the doorway, wearing a sweater and skirt.

"I was just going to clean up when you came," she said.

"Don't give it a thought, Miss Jackes."

* * * *

Ten minutes later I was opening Massey's door, noticing the marks on the lock where someone had tampered with it. Marilyn Jackes had given me the key and told me how to find the place.

At first the living room seemed in order. Then, behind a chair I found a lamp that had been smashed to the floor.

And blood.

I followed a trail of it into a bedroom. Clothes were strewn all over the place. A half-packed suitcase was on the bed. A tennis racket and golf bag lay on the floor near the open door of a closet. Blood stains were everywhere. But no Massey.

It looked as if he had been dragged from the apartment. But not without putting up a terrific fight.

I checked a second bedroom. It seemed long out of use.

There were no other clues to Massey so I got out of there fast and drove hard for Kim's place.

I was shoving up the steps to the entrance when I saw a white Cadillac convertible roll past. The driver didn't see me, but I saw him.

Tanno!

The Caddy turned a corner sharply and I decided it was too late to follow. I flew into the elevator and seconds later I was pounding on Kim's door. There was no answer, so I kept right on pounding. After a long time and weakly, "Who is it?"

I damn near fell dead with relief.

"It's Rod Striker, Kim."

"Say it again."

"It's still Rod Striker. Open up!"

She did. With a rattle of chain. She grabbed me and held on tight for a moment.

"I wanted to make sure it was your voice, Rod. Because about five minutes ago someone else was out there." She closed and locked the door, fixing the chain.

"Know who it was, Kim?"

She shook her head, biting her lip. "I called out but no one answered. So I didn't open. I was too scared."

"Smart," I said. "It could have been Tarino. And if not, you can expect him."

"Expect him? Why?"

"Because I just saw him go by."

"Oh Lord, what'll I do?"

"Nothing. I'll handle it."

She paced, rubbed her temples, sat on the arm of a chair.

"What about Howie?" she said in a tremulous voice. "You haven't said a word."

"I haven't had a chance."

"Is there any news? I can see by your face it's not good. Oh please, tell me quickly!"

"No," I said. "I'm afraid it's not good. I have a couple of ideas, but I'm not sure. So I'll have to call the police."

"The police?" She paled. "Then you didn't find a trace of him?"

"I went to his apartment, Kim. It was a mess. There was evidence of… Well, I think he's in serious trouble."

"My God, what kind of trouble!"

I was trying to think how to put it when there was a sound at the door. I wasn't very surprised, I was expecting something of the kind.

I motioned her towards the bedroom. "Lie on the bed in the dark," I whispered. She seemed paralyzed but I gave her a little shove and she went I cut the lights and quietly removed the door chain. Then I bellied down behind the sofa, the .38 in my hand.

There was the scrape of metal on metal. Slowly the door opened. The gun came first and then the shadow behind it stepped in quickly and closed the door in one soundless motion.

For an age, he stood perfectly still. I knew he was adjusting to the darkness. I didn't breathe. He moved haltingly in my direction, paused, turned towards the bedroom.

I had my shoes off and I followed close behind with the .38 in my fist. He stepped to the bedroom doorway, froze. Slowly he lifted the gun and aimed at the still outline of Kim Massey on the bed.

That was when the butt of my .38 came down on the back of his head. He staggered but didn't fall. He turned the gun on me and I knocked it out of his hand with one downward swipe. Then Kim got the light on and I hooked his jaw with a solid right.

He collapsed and I picked up his gun.

A .32 automatic.

Kim was down on her knees above him, looking up at me and saying over and over, "What have you done, what have you done? Why it's Howie!"

"Sure," I said. "And this .32 he was carrying is the one that killed your aunt You were next."

"He killed my aunt? Howie killed Aunt Martha!"

"That's right."

"Why, why?"

"Your aunt left you her money, didn't she?"

"Yes, but—"

"And did you make out a will in favor of Howie-boy?"

"Yes. We both made out wills the day we were married, each in favor of the other. He insisted, in case anything— Oh God, oh God," she moaned. "How did you know?"

"I didn't know anything for sure. This morning I decided it had to be you or Massey. I thought it was you. Then I went over to Marilyn Jackes place and I saw someone go down her fire escape. The guy looked like Massey and I figured he and Jackes had a thing going together. But when I got to Massey's apartment it was a shambles and covered with blood. He had faked a fight but it convinced me and I didn't know what to think. Except that maybe the guy on the fire escape wasn't Massey at all. Then I saw Tarino and after that I was so goddamn confused I had to play it by ear. Period. Any more questions, ask Massey. He's waking up."

Massey had come to a sitting position, his eyes glazed. I held my gun on him while I moved to the phone and dialed Ben Ulrich.

Kim's face had gone wild. "You killed her, you killed her!" she screamed at Massey. Then she began to pound him with angry little fists. That didn't bother him so she clawed his face with vicious swipes, like a frenzied cat, sobbing the whole time.

I went right on telling Ulrich what had happened.

I didn't once try to stop her.

CHAPTER TWENTY-FOUR

"You mean to tell me," said Myra, "that Tarino had nothing what-soever to do with it?"

"Wrong," I answered. "He got the ball rolling for Massey."

We were in Myra's apartment She was seated across from me, wearing nothing but a robe and one of those flimsy half-nightgowns. A shortie, I guess you call them. I saw it when she came to the door and the robe fell open just enough.

It was a couple of hours later. Massey had confessed and they had booked him. No bail for that boy.

"What kind of double-talk is this?" Myra asked. "Tarino got the ball rolling. I don't read you, Sherlock."

"I only know what I heard the man say down at the station, sweet-heart. According to Massey, he just picked up where Tarino left off."

I took a long swallow of my highball. How I needed that drink! Myra held the robe tight and crossed her legs in such a way that you couldn't see item one.

"I get it," she said. "Tarino gave Massey the idea, but for his part, Tarino was only bluffing."

"Right. Tarino did send a couple of boys to rough Massey up. He did have one of those hoods make the threatening calls. Even though he'll deny it. But he never meant to have anyone killed."

Myra produced a cigarette and I jumped to give her a light. It gave me a chance to nibble her ear and peek at a couple of things that weren't entirely hidden.

"Just how far *did* Tarino take it?" she asked when I finally made it back to my chair.

"Tarino arranged the one and only beating of Massey," I said, "and the calls. Nothing more. Massey lied about someone trying to get into his apartment the night Mrs. Rumshaw was murdered. He scraped the lock himself. He phoned the police to make it look good."

"And he faked the gory scene at his apartment, the one you found tonight?"

"True."

"So what was his little plan?"

"Well, he was gonna shoot Kim, then run and hide somewhere. Later he would claim he was kidnapped but he got away. He wanted to make it appear that he wasn't even around when wifey was killed."

"Did this Marilyn Jackes have anything to do with it?"

"She was playing love games with Massey and that's all. She didn't know his scheme. And his problem was money, first, last and always. He had made a mess of the old man's business. It was deep in the red and be was holding that imported bug-trap together with chewing gum, for show. End of story. Except that I got suspicious after the Aunt was killed. Because unless Kim was in with Tarino, how in the name of Jesus would he expect that she would fall into his arms after he had her aunt knocked off? Unless he was a moron studying to be an idiot, he'd know it was the end of him so far as Kim was concerned.

"Take that line of reasoning and you could only guess that—one, Tarino didn't have the old gal plugged at all, or two, that he did and Kim was on the sidelines applauding all the way. Since Kim had the hots for Eddie-boy in the beginning, I figured she just never cooled off. So I was wrong. Come on over to my little chair and punish me."

"I can throw things from here," said Myra. "God," she sighed. "Dancing virgins on a hot tin roof. I make a big play for Tarino who turns me over to Nick Markos, who dangles me by one foot like a kewpie doll fifteen stories in the air, no parachute—and now you tell me that Massey was our boy all the time."

"What the hell. You got your jollies out of it."

That was when she threw the ice cube at me. But I caught it and tossed back. A lucky pitch. Because the robe was open at the top and it went down her neck. She did a sitting broad jump and landed on her feet. That caused some mighty interesting angles to become exposed.

She glared at me.

I leered back.

She smiled. Then she began to laugh.

"I'm hungry," I said.

"How about a one-inch steak with—"

"We'll eat later," I said, and got to my feet.

She backed off slowly, then she began to run. I chased her all over the goddamn apartment But I guess I wasn't trying very hard.

Because she finally caught me.

ABOUT THE AUTHOR

Robert Colby says: "I began writing while in the South Pacific, invading Jap-held islands with the Army Infantry during World War II. After the war I wrote hit-or-miss for a year or two, then began to study, take private lessons, and attend creative writing courses. I wrote on-and-off for about seven years before I sold my first story to a magazine that promptly collapsed just after sending me a check!

"I then began to write novels and made my first sale, a novel, to Ace Books. Meanwhile, I held down a radio and TV announcer's job at various stations around the country—NBC in New York, CBS in Hollywood, KOA in Denver, WBEN in Buffalo, and WAVE in Louisville, to name a few. Most of the time I would announce half the night and write all the next day. For the past four years I have been writing full time. My wife and I live in a house on the banks of New River in Fort Lauderdale, Florida, one room of which has been converted into an office."

www.ingramcontent.com/pod-product-compliance
Lightning Source LLC
Chambersburg PA
CBHW022034170626
46808CB00003B/1186